The Ghostwriters

by

Mickey J. Corrigan

The Ghostwriters

Contact Information: info@thewildrosepress.com

Cover Art by *Diana Carlile*

The Wild Rose Press, Inc.
PO Box 708
Adams Basin, NY 14410-0708

Visit us at www.thewildrosepress.com

Publishing History
First Crimson Rose Edition, 2016
Print ISBN 978-1-5092-0925-5
Digital ISBN 978-1-5092-0926-2

Published in the United States of America

Dedication

To all the struggling writers still waiting for the muse.

Author Acknowledgments

My thanks to the Ink Well writers group for reading and commenting on earlier versions of this crazy book. You all make me work harder.

Much gratitude to Adam H. Graham, intrepid travel writer and expert on all things Manhattan, for his input on walks around the city.

Deep indebtedness to Athena Sasso, whose ear for thuds and eye for missteps keeps me on the path. Ditto my fearless editor, Diana Carlile.

And thanks to Mel and J.P. for everything. You guys are my everything.

Chapter One

If you really want to know, I met him in a bar. I don't want to go into all of that right now, but there's some stuff you should know.

On February 1, 2010, I was at Collie's Midtown Tavern. Wasted. Again. And trying not to think about how I was, overall, clinically depressed. Late on a Monday night in Manhattan, alone at a crappy bar, fucked up, and...what? Ordering another drink. On top of everything else. The Adderall. The Lexapro. Two sixteen-ounce pale ales, after a high-octane brown bag on the way over. Would I never learn?

That's when JD appeared. He came out of nowhere and rescued me from my sorry-ass self. Handsome, charming, mature. Not something a girl like me could ignore, not in any state of inebriation. And I've experienced them all. Swirling around in some guy's loft bed, wondering what his name was. Head first in a deep-dish toilet at an Upper East Side charity event. Buzzed after a one-night stand, running down Park Ave, lacy underwear clutched in my poorly manicured hands. I've done a lot of crazy things. Whatever.

But JD? He tipped his smooth head my way and gave me the stink eye. Frowned and wriggled his heavy brows. As if to say, "Come, come, sweetheart. Must you let yourself down like this?" I couldn't help it. I sat up straight on my bar stool without ordering that third round. Self-conscious, I ran a hand through my tangled hair, smoothed down my T-shirt. My mind, however, was a mess.

"Help," I said in a drunken whisper-voice.

"Hello, beautiful," he said right back. "Anything I can do? May I suggest a cup of strong black coffee, perhaps?"

He had me from hello. I had him from help.

He talked like my grandfather, all wordy and stiff, but with a snarky little smirk. Like he knew better. Which he absolutely did. Who didn't know better than me in February of 2010?

"C'mon. Grab your purse, child. We'll go up the block to a café. I'll buy you a double espresso."

Dark hair, nice straight-line Jewish nose, wide-open smile. Lively eyes with thick black lashes. An El Greco profile, a George Clooney air of sophistication. How bad could he be? I'd run track all the way through my teens, so if the guy went rogue on me, I'd ditch him in a flash. Half-smashed or not, I was faster than sexy grandpa.

"I am not your grandfather," JD said without me even opening my mouth. "I'm your personal savior. Here to pull you off the bottom of that cesspool you seem to be drowning in. Come, come. Let's get you that caffeine."

Weird. Uncanny. But so what? I let him rescue me. Why not? I was tired of my waste of a life. A little TLC was surely welcome. Some sage grown-up advice? Bring it.

Hey, I'd had ample time to rescue myself. My life had been swirling around and around, whirlpooling in a dirty backwash before sucking itself down the drain.

Can't say I did anything productive or brave to stop my downward spiral. In fact, I'd have to say I pushed things sewer-ward until I heard a satisfying, final sounding slurp.

Me, going under.

We made our way through the crowded bar. Collie's was an old-school watering hole, a Chelsea landmark. On weeknights, it was wall-to-wall local color. Working guys and girls, off-duty firemen and cops, college kids and regular stiffs. Mixed in with a spattering of those phony hipsters from Brooklyn and the sports and gambling crowd. Typically several thick, yowling packs of loosed-up office workers and the obvious regulars, the boozed destitute. Hard-core drunks squeezed along the age-cracked bar.

I'll let you guess where I fit in.

"You should never take candy from strangers," JD said as we pushed through the thick oak door, out into the frigid night. "But this time, you did the right thing."

What candy? What strangers? Was he referring to himself? I started to say something, then stopped. No sense taking a header due to lack of focus during inebriation.

In his gentlemanly way, JD held me up, guiding me along. I was all sheets to the wind, so I let him hook his arm in mine as we made our way through the cold night. He seemed sane enough, not a bit threatening. A pleasant change from some of my usual evening companions.

"You look chilled, darling. Should we just duck in here? This little bodega? I'm sure they have adequate coffee. What do you say, Jacy?"

I didn't remember telling him my name. In fact,

except for that initial cry for help and a couple of drunken grunts, I hadn't said anything to him.

I was about to ask what the fuck when he laughed out loud. "Jacy McMaster. J.C. McMaster. Author of no books, McMaster of none. Of course I know your name."

If I hadn't been so out of it, I would have pushed him away. I would have quick split on the guy. What a rude bastard. And how did he know I'd been struggling to publish a novel? How could he know that? Maybe we'd met before, one drunken night. Maybe he was someone from my blackout past.

Ugh. Now, I wanted to disappear.

But since neither my limbs nor my critical judgment was totally under my control, I held as steady as possible in such conditions. I leaned on his skinny arm and allowed him to gently maneuver me up to the door of the bodega. We peered in. A dozen round tables, no customers. Just a pudgy man with a fat mustache, reading a magazine behind a stainless steel cash register.

A cheesy strip of overhead bells jingled while JD held the door for me. As I wobbled through, he said, "I know everything there is to know about you, Jacy. Everything that matters."

Before I could tell him he was creeping me out, JD handed me a fifty-dollar bill. "Go buy yourself a coffee, child. Then come sit with me, over there by the window."

I let go of his arm and, miraculously, remained standing.

He looked me up and down. "Boy, do I have a job for you."

I was weaving a little, trying to capture the fully upright position and maintain it.

He chattered on. "I'm going to ask for your assistance. Your writing expertise." He raised those bushy brows. "I'm pretty sure you'll help me out and, in the long run, help yourself. Lift yourself out of this…this rut you're in."

Rut? Well, that was as good a word as any to describe the social and psychological void I'd pinballed into.

I took his money and headed for the man behind the counter. When the guy glanced up from his copy of *Girls Go Wild: San Juan*, there was nothing alive in his face. I felt like slapping him back to life. Instead, I ordered a cup of coffee and two chocolate chip muffins. In case JD was hungry.

Of course, I pocketed the change. If JD actually knew everything about me, well then, he already knew I was a terrific liar. A pathological liar and a thief. A cheat and a failure. A cheap date with a bad attitude and too much school debt. He knew I was desperate. That was probably what drew him to me. He could smell it on me.

But he was right about the job lure. I'd probably go for it. I could help him out with his writing project and pocket the change. Fifty dollars toward a cup of coffee? My kind of client.

As soon as I sat down across from him in the uncomfortable metal chair, JD said, "You and I have a number of things in common. One being your gorgeous head. We both reside somewhere inside there. For now."

The fuck? I took a greedy bite out of the bigger

muffin while waiting for the coffee to cool. My phone buzzed, so I scooped it out of my purse and set it on the plastic tablecloth. Red and white checked. Was nothing original anymore?

The text was from Austin, my ex. I still slept with him, but officially he was no longer my boyfriend. When he texted or called, usually after midnight, we were on again. In between, it was over for us. My behavior with Austin disgusted me, but what about my life didn't? Not much.

"In my head?" I asked between wolfish bites. "What does that mean?"

The man behind the counter slapped down his magazine. He stared at me, like I'd interrupted his scholarly pursuits. I smiled, revealing the blobs of chocolate I could feel sticking to my teeth. Counter Man shook his head and went back to his soft porn.

JD leaned in. "It means, Jacy, that I am coming to you via the booze train you so eagerly climbed aboard earlier tonight. Alcohol is a gateway drug. Gateway to the other realms, the otherworldly dimensions. Out there, as they say. Well, you opened the gate, and I slipped in. Now we're taking the ride together." A flicker of a smile dusted his thin lips. "By the way, I'm JD."

How come I already knew that? I shook my head to clear it, but everything remained gauzy.

He flashed a real smile. Perfectly straight teeth, and pretty darn white for a guy his age. "But you already know my name, don't you?" he said. "My full name."

He watched me unpeel the wrapper from the second muffin. His full name, eh? I puzzled over that, the way drunks do with simple statements that loom

6

large enough to supersede the idea of yet another drink. After a minute, I let it go. Who cared? I'd scored the day's best meal, plus forty-odd in change. I wasn't into the details. The muffins were delicious.

"Your favorite book of all time—*The Watcher in the Sky*. Am I right?" He reached across to swipe some muffin crumbs from my chin.

I stopped gorging and looked him in the eye. How the hell did he know that about me? Lucky guess?

"You're a little slow tonight, Jacy. If you're going to help me, we can't have that. I'll need you to be sharp. Real sharp. Which means you'll have to clean up your act."

"Help you do what, exactly?" In the empty room, my voice sounded ridiculously loud.

Mr. Soft Porn flicked his head up and called out, "Hey. None a that now. Take you crazy stuff outside."

JD leaned forward. "Help me write the best book since *The Watcher in the Sky*, Jacy. The longed-for sequel. Tell the story of what happened to the beloved main character after his breakdown. What happened to him when he completed his treatment at the mental health facility and re-entered the phony world that had driven him insane."

"You're nuts," I said with a laugh.

The man behind the counter barked, "You the nutcase. Okay, okay, I close up. Out, out!"

He waved his dirty magazine at us until I stood up, easing my chair back. I was still kind of woozy.

"I close now. You, out." His face was flushed. He swung the magazine like a fly swatter. I could see the glossy images of silicone breasts folded over naked...other things.

I waved back at him and smiled. "We'll leave you alone with your paper girlfriends, dude. Leaving right now." I grabbed my coffee cup and swigged the dregs. "You coming?" I asked JD.

"No, I not coming. Go now, or I call cops," the nosy cashier yelled.

What a freak.

JD smiled a little. "I'll be at your place tomorrow. Think about my offer. I know it's screwy, but it's a big opportunity. Sorry to be clichéd, but it's a chance to grab the gold ring. You don't get a visit from a dead celebrity every day, kiddo. Famous author bearing gifts? Free pass to a future of fame and fortune? This is a once in a lifetime, my girl."

"Thanks for the coffee," I managed to say to JD. My head was full of loose ends I was sure wouldn't tie together until after I'd had at least ten hours of deep sleep. And a long, hot, late afternoon shower.

"You're welcome," Mr. Soft Porn said. "Now go."

So I did.

Chapter Two

When I woke up the next day, I felt terrible. My eyes were swollen shut, so I had to tumble out of bed and crawl through clustering dust devils to the bathroom. I'd suffered worse hangovers after overindulging, but there was a real sharp edge to this one. When I steamed my eyes open with a hot washcloth, I noticed it right away.

Shit. I was still hallucinating.

"You look bad, Jacy, my girl," JD said from his cross-legged perch on my wicker laundry hamper. "First thing we need to do is ease back on the hard-core boozing."

I screamed once or twice before he uncrossed his spidery limbs and said, "Don't be a ninny. You know who I am, that I come from you. From your own deranged mind. So what's the sense of yelling, disturbing your neighbors?"

He had a point. I calmed a little. "You may be an illusion, my illusion. But that sure as fuck does not mean you can stay in my bathroom while I shower."

He shrugged and brushed by me on his way out. "I'll make coffee. And when you come out, all fresh and bright-eyed, we'll discuss how I can save you. Help dislodge you from your habitual cycle of wanton, destructive choices. No more dabbling. Time for you to shed your loser image, child. It is high time. Take my word."

Under the hot pressure of full-blast steamy water, my befuddlement began to clear. And I had to admit, JD was right. About a number of things. I was a major loser, and my lifestyle was epic fail. In the parlance of our times, I was one of those self-destructive creatives. Too much pity-partying, not enough income or success. A lot of wasted time on useless sheeple. Lately, my social life and work output had both been on an unusually steep decline. Maybe I needed the kind of assist a delusion could provide. And what better delusion for a struggling writer than the presence of one of modern America's best-loved novelists?

I shampooed my hair. What if I thought of JD as my muse? That would sure be easier than recognizing the truth about him, about us. I rinsed and conditioned. Why not go with the flow?

Since you're reading this, you must be one of my loyal readers. Or his. Congratulations, you are a revered member of a global minority. Most people don't give a shit about books unless they're translated to film or they include mucho gory violence perpetrated by bloodthirsty killers. Or kinky sex between willing virgins and their crop-wielding bosses, those beloved alphas with hairless chests and six-pack abs. Reading other stuff, literary books for example, is widely regarded as sissy or lame. But you, you actually care about the written word. My heart goes out to you, fellow outlier.

I get you, see. I do. I totally get it. You have an active mind. You love to escape reality. You're inventive, a dreamer. You may even toy with the idea that you, too, could be a writer. You're pretty sure that, if you were to take up the novelist's pen, it wouldn't take too long until you were invited for a live chat with Oprah. Or NPR. Charlie Rose. After all, you have amazing ideas. The journey from here to bestseller, how far can it be? All you need, really, is a good computer program with editing software and a couple of vacation weeks. You'd sit right down and just do it. Hack out the whole damn thing. Instant bestseller. Right?

Right. We all think like that. Until you actually try to write a fucking novel. And then, holy shit. This writing gig, it's fucking hard.

You keep at it. And at it. After days, weeks, months, or—in my sorry-ass case—years of sitting at the keyboard, it finally starts to dawn on you: something is wrong. Still, you keep fighting the good fight. Working hard in obscurity, day after fucking day. Until you get stuck. You encounter a block. A trough of despair. An especially long, completely unproductive stretch, one that drags on and on.

Suddenly, reality strikes. You're done. And it doesn't even matter because you suck. Your writing sucks.

Truth hurts. Ouch. Your reflection in the literary mirror is hideous. You, you're no fiction badass. You're anon. As in anonymous. Obscure. Mediocre would be a step up, a blessing. Once you see yourself as you are, well, it's pretty much all over. You can't even write bad fiction anymore. And your fantasy of becoming a bestselling author? Totally doomed.

Hey, I eventually learned this ugly truth. Finally, I got it. But first, I earned a useless undergrad degree in English Lit, running up a loan tab higher than I could ever pay back as a high school English teacher. Not satisfied with that level of debt, I had to boost the ante. Eight torturous months later, I dropped out of a sadistic graduate program in creative writing. Those people nearly killed me. After a short recovery period, I sat myself down at the unfinished pine door I'd set on top of a couple of empty file cabinets. And I began pecking away. Day after useless day. Page after unpublishable page. Two years of this self-abuse with nothing to show for it. Nothing worthwhile, anyway.

All of a sudden, I was older, tired. Were those actual wrinkles around my eyes? Crow's feet already? I'd developed a tiny paunch at the waist. A deep love of Red Bull and vodka, consumed on foot while on the way to dirty watering holes. Bad habits galore. For good reason. I was twenty-fucking-four and still virtually unpublished. The lit mag from your alma mater doesn't count. Angry letters to the editor of local alternative newspapers, those don't count either. Here I was, a weekend waitress at the Big Brewdha Microbrewery, making shitty money, throwing it away. All week long, drinking up my hard-earned dough. Mainly at the local pick-up bars and quintessential drinking dives like Collie's.

Yes, there I was, right on the self-cutting edge of giving up. Because I'd finally grasped hold of that ugly truth—my writing was going nowhere.

Why? Because it sucked.

Truth is, most people's writing sucks. It didn't help me, knowing this. I wasn't most people. I was the next big thing. Or nothing.

Nothing seemed a hundred percent likely. Drinking eased the pain. One-night stands with a string of nameless men. Some mean. Some downright scary. I took no names. More anon for me. Too much booze, prescription meds, a few hits of this, of that. The sewer beckoned. I fell in. Head first. Head down.

Then JD. The booze train ran me over, then somehow rode me out of the skanky darkness and JD was there. And here he was still, in my one-bedroom Midtown apartment. So, either I had to admit I was on a permanent headtrip and facing a bleak future as a complete lunatic. Not an acceptable option. Or else I could take full advantage of his mysterious presence. Take JD up on his offer. Go for it, and let his illusionary self do what he said he wanted to do—show me how to write a sequel to my all-time favorite novel. One of the most revered coming of age stories in the history of American literature.

What would you choose, my book-loving friend? A swift run to the local headshrinker for a prescription for the latest in antipsychotics? Or an internship with an American classic? Hey, everybody loves a dead icon, right?

When I opened the bathroom door, wrapped in a fluffy pink towel, I smelled my Mexican dark roast. And toaster pastries, caramel frosted. My ghostly writer had made me breakfast.

How bad could this be?

Not as bad as you might think. Not at first. Bit of a sand dune to mount, then the glorious beach spread out in front of you. That's how life always is—the sun so lovely, golden, warming you gently on the pure white sands of paradise. Before it burns the tender skin right off your sorry ass.

Stretched out on my saggy, black leather couch, JD looked comfortable, but he overpowered the small room. Just like my couch did. And he seemed out of place. His clothes were rural New Hampshire circa 1968. He looked like somebody's sitcom dad. I scuttled into my bedroom to pull on some clothes. I could feel his eyes on me, those dark dead man's eyes.

"Don't be ridiculous, Jacy. My eyes are lively. At least, you thought so last night."

I slammed my door. The mind reading thing was annoying. And he was old. I had an old man in my head. And in my apartment.

"Old man," I heard him say. "That's a load of crap."

When I came out a few minutes later, dressed in jeans and a long shapeless sweater, he was gone.

****

Austin called before I could pour my first drink of the day. I'd napped for a few hours in front of the TV, then pigged out on cold Pop-Tarts. I was headed for the wine rack when my phone buzzed. I let it go to voice mail, just to let him suffer a little.

Of course, I returned Austin's call. Right after I popped the cork on a bottle of Chilean red. I didn't want to suffer too long myself. The crappy hangover was bad enough. I needed a pick-me-up. Like some friendly male company. Live male company.

"Yo, baby. Whaddup?" I kept my voice light, so he wouldn't think I was excited he'd actually called before the witching hour.

Austin cleared his throat the way he always did when he disapproved of me. He did this a lot, unless we were in bed together. Then he'd make other kinds of sounds. Which is what kept him coming back for more. I'm no fool. I knew he didn't love me for my scintillating intellect or my sweet personality.

"Where were you last night?" he scolded. "I rented a movie. Thought you might want me to come by."

Since when had we watched a movie together? It was wham, bam, a snore, and a shower for the two of us. We'd been like that for more than a year, ever since he'd fallen for the whore who shall remain nameless. Okay, Shari. All tits and no smarts, that Shari. What did she have that I didn't? Oh yeah: Austin.

"Sorry, Aus. I had company. Couldn't answer the phone."

I was always trying to make him jealous, but he wasn't capable of taking a hint. As usual, he asked no questions, letting the reference to another man pass. On to more important things—himself.

"I'm horny. I need my Jacy fix, babe, or I won't be able to sleep tonight. I have to look tight tomorrow. We're in court at nine. So listen, what're you doing right now? Still have time on the movie rental. I can come by."

Hangovers make me meaner than usual, which is mean enough. With a big head and a bad taste in my mouth, I can be yard dog mean.

"Where's Shari been lately? Doesn't she like to watch movies with you before you go prosecute some innocent person? Send them away to some awful prison, where they'll get hep C and butt fucked?" I dug the blade in deep, ready to twist and shout. Movies? Come on. I wasn't sure, but with Austin, talk of watching movies was probably prep school code. For whipping out the fur-lined handcuffs or, most likely, watching porn while you were going at it. "Why don't you call Shari at the last minute? See what she says when you tell her you need to screw somebody and she'll have to do?"

He laughed. "You were at Collie's last night, huh." Austin wasn't asking. He could tell I was hung over. "Listen, hon, I'll pick up a bottle on my way over. See you in twenty."

I missed the days when you could slam down a phone receiver. Now you would only hurt yourself. You couldn't even toss your cell across the room, smashing it against a cement wall. Because who wanted to wait in that endless line at the provider outlet? Not me. I gave my phone a careful underarm pitch. It landed in the steep pile of dirty laundry stacked on the dish drain next to the sink.

"Beautiful," JD said.

I nearly jumped out of my skinny jeans. He lounged across the couch, his thin torso sinking into the indentations I'd so recently left behind.

"Did you know you forgot that silly little gadget at the bodega last night?" He smirked. "See? I brought your phone home for you. Figured you'd need it to catch up with your boyfriend. So he can come over, give you the time."

He was flashing me one of those knowing looks, the kind you get from older men when boyfriends are the topic of discussion. Still, I did need my phone. I remembered placing it on the table. I didn't recall putting it back in my purse. So what could I say to JD?

"Um, thanks." I sighed. "I guess I can help you out with your project."

"Beautiful," he said again. He actually looked enthusiastic. "Too late to get anything done today, though. We'll get started tomorrow." When I shrugged,

16

careless, he turned serious. "Please. Just a few drinks tonight, nothing more. Have your fun with lover boy, but do get a good night's sleep. I like to work in the early mornings. That's when I have the best energy."

Whatever. "So, how much you paying me for this freelance job?"

He frowned. "You'll get your pay, Jacy. More money than you can imagine. More money than the *Fifty Shades of Perversion* author, or that British woman who did the silly magic school books. More than the one with the trashy young vampires series." He shivered. "Please. But you work with me, and you'll make more money than those three dilettantes put together."

I wondered why he was only comparing me to female writers. Was lousy bestseller status a gender thing?

Before I could ask, he added, "Seriously, though, I can't promise your writing will be widely respected like, say, Franzen or Rushdie. But Jacy, you'll be light-years beyond mediocrity. You'll be published, successful, famous. Okay?"

What fledgling writer is going to say no to that pitch?

"Okay," I said, but grudgingly. Because I got the distinct feeling he was a goddam sexist.

He pointed to my bookcase and smiled. "I see you have some important works on your shelves. My friend Pynchon. Mailer. Vonnegut. Camus. Kerouac, he was soulful. Toni Morrison, yes. And Plath, she had quite the voice. Fante. Now there was an unrecognized genius." JD nodded and glanced at me. "But do you really read this other crap? Wallace? Eggers? And this

Hornby fellow? Why do you read this nonsense? To learn what not to do?"

I shrugged. I'd read a lot of books because it was required of me. The books I loved most were stacked on the floor next to my bed. *The Watcher in the Sky*, for one. Gatsby. Everything by Bret Easton Ellis, Joy Williams, and Haruki Murakami. But I didn't want to discuss my taste in fiction with JD. So I didn't. And he let it go.

"Look," he said, "the project itself won't be difficult. I can see us putting it together in a matter of days. Because mostly you'll be typing and I'll be dictating. Yours is more of a secretarial position, actually." He saw the look on my face and added, "Yes indeed, I am an admitted sexist. But you do have a role in this project, Jacy. An essential role. Boy oh boy. Transcribing material dictated from the other side? This is something few mortals can do. I ought to know. I was one of the rare ones."

Huh? Who was he kidding? But he held up a hand when I started to interject.

"Look. Booze didn't do it for me. I had to reach out to the other realms via other means. Celibacy, fasting, meditation. Which didn't always work. But when it did? The results were paradigm shifting." His smile sparkled with proud self-belief.

What an ego. Wow. Paradigm shifting? Huh. One American novelist's personal influence on global social trends seemed, overall in the scheme of human history, pretty fucking minor. His view of his own cultural impact was wildly exaggerated. And what about all the serial killers who toted his book around when they went on their bloody sprees? Maybe that was what he meant by paradigm shifting.

I wasn't sure, but it seemed to me JD's work might not have had the kind of social effect he was claiming for himself. But certainly, he'd had his say. His writing was immensely popular. After almost sixty years, his books were all still in print. And they were still selling. So he'd had something. That was for sure.

JD nodded, as if in agreement with my thoughts. "Yes indeed. And they don't stop liking you after you're dead, either." He shrugged, trying to appear humble. "After all, the act of writing can be equivalent to a personal search for enlightenment. So, when it comes to you from the higher realms, your readers know it. And your book sales reflect that. And how."

Maybe so. But taking dictation from a ghost? I sipped my wine, looked away. I wasn't that swift as a typist. Mine was more of a hunt-and-peck style.

He picked up on my discomfort. "Don't worry, kiddo, we'll iron out the details. Our work together will flow smoothly, I can assure you. I've got the manuscript done. It's already been written, so it's just a matter of creating an edited version. One with a physical presence. Then we submit it to publishers. Under your name, of course."

I winced. JD smiled in commiseration. I didn't have to say what I was thinking. Fuck New York publishers. Bunch of sadistic creeps. I'd tried to interest them in proposals for my never-finished novels. But I'd had no luck with those bastards. No luck at all.

JD crossed his legs and continued with his predictions. "With this book of ours, you'll have no trouble finding a literary agent. And a decent publishing house."

I wanted to believe him. Like a degenerate gambler at a Vegas casino copping a loan from a greasy shylock. Sinking my life ever deeper in the shit. But hey, writing is like that. Every book you write is going to be the big winner. The pot of gold, the all-in hand. Every book is the one that'll make you rich. Put you on the map. Save your sorry ass. Rescue you from the banal human state of nobodyness.

And here I'd thought I was past all that. Hadn't I almost fully accepted the reality of my indisputable literary suckiness?

I had. I really had. But now I faced a splendid opportunity to forget that monster-in-the-mirror truth.

He leaned forward. "This one won't be like all the rest, Jacy. No nasty rejections. No stock refusals. It's an easy in. You'll be famous in no time." He paused while my weak ego licked itself all over. Then he frowned, bringing all his facial creases into stark relief. "But there will be demands you'll have to deal with. A book this important will necessitate a fair amount of public flattery. They'll commodify your life, and you'll be caught up in the publicity machine. With all of their moronic promotional endeavors and all that phony marketing bullshit."

He shook his head. He had one of those oversize heads like a governor or a TV commentator. Too big for his narrow shoulders. "You'll be on your own with all that. I'm no good at that kind of thing. Especially now that I'm, well, dead." He stared into space for a moment, then shook his huge head again. "In a few years, most likely there will be misleading 'biographies' and silly films about me, perhaps even some rumors of old manuscripts of mine. That's why your book will need to be published first, to set the record straight. Our work together, this is the important thing."

His face lit up for a moment. "The goddam sequel to *The Watcher in the Sky*. The book everyone has been waiting for. The rest? The rest is just nonsense." His eyes downcast, he admitted, "I didn't leave anything behind worth publishing. And they know it."

JD glanced at me then, scrunched his face, and laughed. Sort of a sad laugh, though. If he hadn't been such a manipulative, obtrusive asshole, I might have felt sorry for him.

"And the rumors about me penning Pynchon's later novels are just that, rumors. Media crap. We've been friends for decades, but the man does his own work. As I've done mine. Like me, Tom interacts with the zeitgeist but does not invest in it. You might think about that when you next take a drink. Or a boyfriend."

Huh? I was not following his line of thinking.

"But this? Our work together? This is the big book, Jacy. Guaranteed bestseller. All you have to do is work with me." His smile was patient and beneficent.

But really? Would it be that easy? I worked on my wine. Guzzled might be the appropriate term. All this talk of big deal books and long-awaited bestsellers unnerved me. Was he full of shit like all men?

Of course, he knew what I was thinking. I guzzled some more. Then we glared at one another. How was this ever going to work, really?

"Remember what I told you about a clear head, child." JD said. "Use some caution tonight. The sooner we get this ball rolling, the sooner you'll be able to stop drinking away your lack of self-esteem."

I chugged what was left in my glass.

"Consider removing this Austin fellow from the equation, will you, dear girl? He's an obstacle. For this boob of yours, this blasé member of the cult of billable hours, to interfere with our work would be a kind of sacrilege. Please think about this tonight when he has his selfish way with you."

What could I say to that? I rolled my eyes and got up to refill my glass.

When the doorbell buzzed, I gave JD the stink eye. He knew what I meant. Out!

By the time I'd finished kissing Austin in the entry hall and dragged him into the living area, JD was gone. I kept looking for him out of the corner of my eye. When Austin undressed me, I felt like covering myself back up. Later, in my bedroom, I pulled the braided afghan over our naked bodies.

My paranoia went unnoticed. Austin was into Austin, not me and my issues.

Of course, we didn't watch a movie. But I didn't do much drinking, either. In fact, we crashed early and, for once, I enjoyed an excellent night's sleep.

When Austin got up to leave around six, I was already wide awake. "Thanks for the mammaries," he said, kissing my breasts goodbye.

One of his juvenile prep school lines. He fondled around like a playful toddler, then headed off for another day of pretending to be an adult. Not sure how he did it, but he raked in a six figure salary at one of the top legal firms in town.

I sat up and ran a hand though my rough-housed hair. JD would be proud. I was as clear headed as I came. Just the way he'd wanted. I wasn't free of entanglements, but at least my mind wasn't turbid.

Full of energy, I jumped out of bed and pulled the sheets tight. I smoothed out the wrinkles in my black cotton bedding and folded the matching afghan. Close enough to a made bed, as close as mine ever got. Domestic duties were not my forte.

Padding across the hardwood floor, I hummed tunelessly. My mood was better than usual, which only meant I wasn't suicidally bleak. If I hadn't been expecting JD to arrive and begin our project, I might have been grousing to myself. He had a point—writing was meditation, men were distractions. The Austin plotline wasn't going anywhere, and I knew it. Used and abused, that was always my story with men. All my life—same old, same old. Me for sex, not me for love. I wasn't sure why I slept with them. Austin was no different.

In the shower, I wondered if JD would turn out to be just like the rest of them. Men. They were always lying to me. Acting infantile. Seeing me as a sex object. Bossing me around, treating me bad, casting me aside, and bruising what was left of my flimsy ego. I shaved my legs. That's when I remembered JD couldn't do anything to hurt me. He wasn't physical. He was all in my mind.

When I opened the bathroom door, I was whistling something that resembled a tune. It could have been *Crazy* by Patsy Cline. Maybe not. I'm not musical. I don't have a head for lyrics.

"I took the liberty of firing up your computer. Coffee's on. Come, come."

I jumped at the voice from across the room. My bath towel slipped a bit but, thank god, remained mostly in place.

JD had settled in a tumble-down vinyl chair he'd dragged out from under my three-legged kitchen table. He sat there calmly, right beside my empty office chair, in front of my messy desk. My desktop wallpaper flashed a series of color photos—me and Austin on the beach at Nantucket, Mother and Daddy in front of their brownstone, my brother Jerome clutching a massive chess trophy with a huge grin on his face.

JD tapped his fingers on a legal pad next to the computer. Hot steam escaped in wisps from my morning mug. The white and red one that said, "Cultivate Randomness."

Hugging my bath towel close, I said, "Nine is a better time for me to begin my day. But hang on. Give me a minute to get dressed."

The man was rude and annoying. I mean, really. He had to stop popping in any time he felt like it. It was barely seven o'clock. But a small smile crept across my lips. What the hell, right?

"That's my girl," JD said.

For a moment there, we felt like a team.

Chapter Three

The first couple days of working together were rough. Communication between two people is always difficult. Especially between men and women. Older folks and young people? Not easy. Dead guys and live girls? Big challenge.

The way I saw the problem was this—JD was old-school; I'm post-postmodern.

He saw it differently—he was the genius; I was an unreliable, silly, pain in the ass female.

Sexism aside, probably there was some truth to both of our opinions. Whatever. Each morning began the same way—hot coffee, wary smiles, seated together at my desk. And every morning ended the same way—both of us yelling, me tossing pencils and crumpled balls of notebook paper around my apartment, him storming out, and me popping corks. That's exactly what happened on day one, and day two was nothing but a repeat. We fought like baby animals, kicking and squalling, all flashing tooth and claw. No blood was spilled, but we got very little writing done. Progress had been better when I was on my own. That's how bad it was.

So much for having a muse. So much for hallucinating a ghost writer. Except, technically, I was the ghostwriter. He was the ghost writer.

In the early afternoon of our second day, after four

stressful hours of head-to-head combat, I wandered into the kitchen for a badly needed shot of frozen vodka. He'd called my dialogue "putrid," my verb choices "mushy turds." My hands were shaking when I hefted the icy Stoli bottle to my lips.

He clucked his disapproval. Fuck him. "To escape," I scoffed. My standard toast. Glug glug.

"Suave as hell, Jacy," he said.

I was steaming. So I lunged. "Are you sure you're dead? When exactly did you bite the dust? I mean, you act like a regular asshole, just like a live guy."

JD sat back in his chair and stared at me. His expression was mildly disturbing, a mix of puzzlement and insane anger.

"I died two days before we met at that Chelsea hellhole you so foolishly frequent. Where, may I remind you, your lovely head was completely wrecked." He glared. "You were so drunk, so out of your mind, you were open to anything that came along. Fortunately, what came along was me. My recently departed spirit. With reams of brilliant unfinished business. I needed a host, you seemed like a willing hostess. Your call. My decision."

Had it been my call? I didn't remember it that way. I twisted the cap off the Stoli bottle again.

Suddenly, JD smacked the desk with his hand. I jumped, and the vodka sloshed. "Quit boozing yourself, will you? We have work to do!"

Startled into compliance, I tucked the bottle back in the freezer and slammed the creaky door. But his imperious tone bugged the hell out of me. He was really getting under my skin.

Leaning against the fridge, I lashed out, tongue

loosened by my liquid lunch. "No offense, but why don't you stop? Stop acting the way you did before you passed. Cuz hey, I don't need you to run my life the way those other bitches did. I'm not some love-struck fan teen. Ours is a business arrangement, right?" I waited there in the kitchen, watching his dark eyes boil in his supersized head. "No offense," I repeated. As if that might erase the nastiness of my outburst.

"Those other young women? I assume you're referring to my wives and girlfriends? For your information, no matter what you've read in the crappy gossip rags, I did not run their lives. Their silly lives were completely out of control. So I was forced, over and over, to step in and help them. Make sound decisions, bail them out of stupid messes." He shook his head. "Not that this was appreciated, mind you."

I could see why. The man was a control freak, a domineering megalomaniac on a massive ego-trip. Personality flaws that appeared, in his case, to be permanent. Even post-mortem.

I said, "Look. You are here to bring your book to life. Not to take over mine." I wanted to hit the Stoli, hit it again and again, but I didn't want him to be able to use that against me. So I plugged in the coffee-maker to reheat what was left in the pot. "No offense, but your attitude is grade F chauvinism."

He hooted. "If that's what you're rebelling against when I remind you how to punctuate, how to use proper grammar, how to compose a decent sentence, well, that's just childish. I thought I was working with an adult. A seasoned, if not exactly successful, professional."

We were getting into it again. I already knew

where this was headed. There would be no winning with the dead man in my skull. "I guess—"

"You guess correctly," he interrupted. He did this constantly, speed-reading the mind we shared, cutting me off mid-sentence. "Since you can't win, as you say, you need to change your behavior. Quit fighting me. Allow me in. Be an open vessel, allow my words to pour through you. As if you were channeling a wise spirit." His voice lowered to a soft purr, calming my instinct to keep arguing. "You've got to quit holding back, Jacy. Let go of the chokehold on your subconscious mind. Set free what's in there—unknown worlds, uncensored words, the excitement of uncontrolled writing. Stop strangling the voice inside you. Let it become your own without beating it senseless and rolling it up in a rug."

He stood up, wandered away from the desk. After a moment, he stopped before the window. The view from my living area was mostly concrete and glass. What you looked at was another nondescript building, a brick apartment high-rise almost exactly like my own.

"Come here." His voice was strange, choked sounding.

The smell of scalding coffee filled the room. I shrugged and joined him at the window. The panes were coated with grime. Life in the big city is dirty. The best dirty fighter usually wins.

"Look at them. Watch how she follows his lead," he ordered.

That's when I saw what he was looking at—the college girl in the apartment across from mine. Her curtains were open and she was putting on quite the show. I rolled my eyes. I'd lost interest in Debbie-

Does-Dull-Guys months ago. After a brief stint with binoculars, I'd cooled on her twenty-four/seven love life.

I turned away. The coffee was burbling.

"You're not doing what I said," JD scolded. "Watch her. There's something you need to learn from this."

Ick. Dirty old men made me ill. Especially dead ones.

I glanced at JD, but he was ignoring my thoughts, his eyes glued to the scene across the alley. With a heavy sigh, I watched Debbie and her latest conquest. As expected, they were half-dressed and getting right down to it. This dull guy was a dark, meaty sort, double Debbie's ballet-girl size. Her back was pressed up against the living room wall while he knelt in front of her, his face at her crotch. Her eyes were closed, her mouth open. The dreamy look on her face shifted as he stood up and entered her, lifting her up the wall with each thrust. She wrapped her matchstick legs around his hairy back. Even from this far away, I could tell her shoes were off the rack.

Yawn. Coed sex against a wall. So? Who hadn't done that old thing? I started to turn away again, my mind drifting. Hey, voyeurism's not my trip. Everybody knows women don't enjoy watching other people fuck. Not as much as men do. It's a known fact. A loving partner turns us on, not someone else's. These things are hard-wired. It's better for species survival or something. Let JD watch them do the nasty. I needed coffee.

"Stay here. I want you to see the way she opens to him, allowing him to merge with her. Become one with her."

JD put his arm around my shoulder and pulled me to him. He hadn't touched me since the night we met. I preferred it that way. His hand on my forearm was cold, chilling my flesh.

"Look at her. She's lost herself in him."

He had a point. The expression on my neighbor's face, the way her head and limbs bounced around as her boyfriend pounded into her. It was like she had no control, no say in what happened to her. Like she'd abandoned herself to something beyond herself.

"She's no longer herself, Jacy. She's his. Part of them. She is them."

He looked down at me, cradled against his stringy torso. "This is what I want for us, Jacy. Unrestrained merging."

Gag. Me and JD? Nope. Not gonna happen. Oh, he was handsome all right and smart. Famous. But he was way too old. And dead.

Too old, too dead. I thought this over and over— too old, too dead, too old, too dead. Until he let go of me, dropping his long arm to his side.

"You don't understand, child. I'm not interested in your body. I'm talking about your mind."

That would be a first. A man who wanted me for my brain? Unlikely. Except that he was, in fact, a part of my brain.

He smiled at me, encouraging. "Exactly. Think of me as the part of your mind you are gripping too tight. The part you are simultaneously pushing away. Boy oh boy, I'm the part of your mind that's up against a wall. And that needs a good fucking."

I laughed. I hadn't expected to hear such language

coming from him.

He instantly corrected that mistake in my thinking. "Remember, dear heart, my novel was for decades the most widely banned book in America. It's still banned globally, not allowed in libraries and schools in some areas of the U.S. Largely because I included the f-word." He grinned. "Fuck. A personal favorite of mine." He paused, reconsidering. "The word, not the action."

As I poured myself a cup of burnt coffee, I remembered what I'd read about JD when I wiki-ed him. His weirdly monastic sexual habits. The semi-pedophilic attitude, the teen brides. No wonder he wasn't interested in my body. I was way past puberty, my virginity "spoiled" by many a night of good hard fucking.

But what he'd said about my mind? That grabbed my interest. Maybe he was onto something. In my writing classes and workshops, my work had been criticized as being overly controlled. Maybe JD was right. That might be what had blocked my writing success the past couple of years. For our partnership to work, could be I'd have to let him take the reins. Ride me hard. Bareback, even.

"I wouldn't have selected that crass metaphor, Jacy." He was seated by my desk again, tapping into my thoughts while waiting for me. "But yes, you need to let go. Let go and let JD." He smiled. "Let me do what I do best." He folded his pale hands in his lap, nodding sagely. "Let me take the lead, and we can work together as one. Take my word. I guarantee the results will be better than anything you could ever do on your own."

This pissed me off. He had a way of twisting everything around so I felt small. Powerless. Inept.

He soothed. "I can't do it without you, kid. I need you. And you need me." Those delving eyes, that penetrating smile. The hypnotic burr of his voice. "Come, come. Open yourself to me. Merge your mind with mine, and see how, together, we can make something. Something incredibly beautiful."

Oh, what the hell. I sat down beside him and clicked open the file we'd been working on, fighting over for two straight days. For what? It was total shit.

I trashed it, opened up a new file. Two sips of gut-wrenching coffee, one deep breath. "Okay, JD," I said. "Hit me with your rhythm stick."

"Pardon?"

I laughed. "Just an expression. What I meant was, I'm ready. Start dictation."

"It will help if you allow your mind to drift a little. Like when you are falling asleep. When you are still half-awake but clear-minded and calm. Aware, but not moored. Still yourself, but open to something else. Wide open."

Closing my eyes, I focused on my breathing. Slowly, my breathing tempered, my heartbeat eased. I could feel myself drifting. Calming. Om. I slid into a kind of Zen place. A dreamlike state.

JD began to talk, to dictate. He spoke to me as to an intimate friend. He spoke casually, at a leisurely pace. I typed along as I listened with my mind's ear, tuning out the import, the content, as he unveiled his story. His beautiful words, they came to me. They flowed through me, one after the other in a sparkling stream.

I typed for hours without stopping. My fingers loped across the keys.

When I saved the file and stood up from my desk, it was dark outside. My wrists were stiff, and my knees were weak. I couldn't remember a single thing I'd typed, not a single sentence. If you'd asked me for the details of our day's work, I would have had to tell you, truthfully, I had no clue.

None.

But this I knew for sure, the work was beautiful. It sang. And the writing was pure bestseller genius.

Chapter Four

You'd think I would've known better. But once JD took a powder and I had the evening to myself, I started on a Bull and Stoli and ended in a stranger's bed.

Typical me. Sometimes I hated myself.

When I woke up, he was curled around me. There we were, a couple of spooning strangers. Ugh.

My head pounded, and my face felt frozen solid. Fortunately, I still had my clothes on. So I thought maybe we hadn't…you know.

He was snoring. His hard dick pressed up against a back pocket of my jeans. Okay, so maybe we had, after all. Maybe I'd put my clothes back on because his place was like a freaking igloo.

I didn't try to recapture the details. Really, I didn't want to know. I was a bit of a shit magnet, to tell you the truth. So sometimes my evenings on the town were, I felt, best left in the black hole part of my brain, untouched. To paraphrase somebody, the unexamined life is worth living. Or something like that.

Carefully, silently, I eased my body away from his. I would tiptoe out, slip away before we were forced to face one another in the harsh light of the day after. Wouldn't be the first time I'd pulled off a middle of the night quick split. Had it happen to me, too, many a time. So long, whatever your name is. Thanks for nothing.

When I lifted his meaty arm off my hip, he rolled over, snorting a few times like big men tend to do. The guy was massive, a linebacker bouncer type. I checked his profile. Cute as hell. A few memories poked through the alcohol clouds. Scottish heritage. Rugby team. Funny.

Too bad I wouldn't be sticking around to check my facts. I felt around for my cowboy boots, hoping they were next to the bed. The floor was cold, damp. Either Mr. Snore had a basement apartment or the place had been recently flooded. Either way, it could've used a little heat.

"Don't leave just yet. I'll make us a cup of tea." His voice low, warm, kind.

I remembered suddenly how much I'd liked talking to him. Firth, his name was Firth. A social worker with the city.

"Can't. I really have to go." A lie, of course.

One boot still eluded me, but now that he was awake, I rustled about in search of it. My ratty suede jacket was draped over the arm of a squat couch, my battered purse beside it. They looked like a couple of homeless people, lying there on the dirt-brown microfiber, side by side.

"You meeting with the author again today?" Firth propped himself up against the scarred headboard. He seemed interested in my response. How quaint. "The old guy, what's his name?"

How much had I spilled? Hopefully, I'd lied the way I always lied—profusely.

I nodded vaguely, avoiding his eyes. "And now I'm late for a meet with the guy."

It was still dark out, so this was an obvious ditch-story. I underlined my deceit by asking him the time while yanking on the missing boot.

"Five. Fer fuck's sake, you always go to work this early? Must be one of those dedicated writers. I'm exhausted but impressed."

When I looked up from my stubborn boot, Firth was smiling at me. Fondly? I'd have to say, yes, with affection. Celtic eyes sparkling. Fire-engine bed-head, bright red-orange hair all over the place. Freckles. A sort of altar boy innocence. Which made me feel like a big ho for running off the way I was. This guy Firth, he seemed sweet. And he seemed to actually like me.

"I'll probably go back to sleep when you leave. Sleep through my alarm. Take shite from my crack-head boss." Firth laughed. "Just another day in government shackles. So, you still up for a drink later on?"

I must have agreed to see him again. Not my usual style, but I did make exceptions now and then. Even after a dozen draft beers, I knew who I liked and who I didn't. Trouble was, I usually liked the wrong guys.

But Firth seemed different, somehow. Sweetly intense. His slight brogue was adorable, his face, too, both as Scottish as a quart of single malt. So what the hell? Maybe I would see how much I enjoyed his company without the misleading glaze induced by shots and schooners.

"Um, yeah, let's meet for that drink."

His grin widened. "Cool. Collie's? Ten?"

I was on my way to the door by then. "Sure. See ya."

Before I could make my escape, however, Firth climbed out of his sagging bed. The man was huge, but not the least bit fat. He was evenly muscled. Pale skin covered with a soft mat of red-gold hair. And standing before me, naked, he was…holy shit, big. Whoa.

He caught me at the front door and grabbed me in a bear hug. "I like you, Jacy," he mumbled in my ear. "You're interesting."

Interesting? That was a new one. I hugged him back. He smelled like a forest, pine needled, mossed and musty. Earthy.

Not bad. I breathed him in. Not bad at all.

Still, I dashed off like I had somewhere more important to be.

Out on the empty street, I shivered in the harsh wind while I checked my phone for missed calls. So many I didn't want to begin retrieving them. Most were from Mother. She'd also sent a text, which I made myself look at. *Come to dinner. Jerome's birthday tomorrow.*

Tomorrow meaning tonight. Shit.

The air was heavy and smelled like snow. I huddled in my thin jacket and headed east to check the cross street. One of these days, I'd buy a warm winter jacket. I'd been telling myself this for the last three years. I was still ignoring myself, though. Like, if I didn't own any winter clothes, I could pretend there wouldn't be much cold weather from October through May. I lived in denial world.

Walking along the deserted sidewalk, I scrolled through the rest of my messages. Nothing from Austin, the prick. I was tempted to call him and announce that I'd met someone real. Someone with a human heart instead of a slick racket and a phony smile. He wouldn't care, though. He'd just laugh, ask if I'd been at Collie's again.

I got my bearings and realized I was in the West Village. Pretty near work, not that far from Collie's and not so many blocks from my place. Firth was practically a neighbor. I slowed down. After all, I was rushing for no reason. I'd made my escape. Nobody was in pursuit. And JD wouldn't be at the computer this early. Why exhaust myself?

The frosty air slapped me around, helping to revive my beer-soaked brain cells. After walking for a while, I felt pretty damn good, considering. I thought about Firth, his kindness, the hug, his big bearish bod. He seemed kind of interesting himself. I was hating myself a little less than usual. Which was sort of pleasant. Maybe my shit magnet had lost its pull?

Less than an hour later, I sat at my desk answering the emails I'd been ignoring for weeks. One of the perks of crashing at a stranger's house—escaping early stretched out the day, allowing me to catch up on everything I normally procrastinate until forced to confront, usually in the form of a crisis. This included paying overdue bills, lying creatively to the college loan people—may they all rot in hell—and freaking over Mitch's work schedule for the Big Brewdha. My manager was an okay guy, but he continually tried to wheedle me into working weeknights. No way. I needed my weeknights for messing myself up, and my debauched lifestyle was dependent on the more generous weekend tips.

Sipping coffee, I responded to the digital onslaught, pushing everyone off for another day or two. What a load of crap. All of it. Don't get me started on how much I detest how we're all expected to communicate twenty-four/seven. Facebook, Twitter, LinkedIn, all that nonsense? I'm a conscientious objector to the Self-Promotion Industrial Complex. Really, it's narcissism gone wild. I hate the hell out of social networking. Now that we all have so many friends, why is it we're all so fucking lonely? And what's with everyone posting a million happy-face photos? Nobody I know is that in love with life. Why are we all pretending so damn hard?

Don't get me started on blogs, either. Everyone thinks they have something to say. And the truth is, most of us don't.

But just out of curiosity, I zipped around i-world, checking on friends. Everyone looked incredibly busy. If you didn't know better, you'd get depressed reading about it. You might feel bad, seeing what productive lives everyone else was leading.

A pot of double-dose Colombian coffee on top of a wild night on top of everyday bullshit stress. By nine o'clock, I wasn't doing so good. Of course, that's when Mother called. Always guaranteed to send me fleeing to the medicine cabinet for happy pills. I was tempted to let her call go to messages, but imprinted infantile guilt won out. I'd been ignoring her for months. Three glorious months without a McMaster guilt trip. Like an island vacation in my own mind.

I took a deep breath. "Hello, Mother."

My hands instantly turned clammy. It was my brother's birthday, so I had to be nice to her. I had to go over for dinner, too. There was no way around that, either. Jerome's birthday? Christ alive. The day was practically a global holiday. An international day of worship. Would the banks be open? Did I need to throw down a prayer rug?

She started right in. "Dinner's at seven. Are you bringing that boy you've been seeing? Dallas?"

"Austin, Mother. Smaller, hipper, less Republican. No, I doubt he can get away. He's in court this week." In court or in Shari. Either way, he wasn't about to join my family for dinner.

"Hmph. Well, come along by yourself then. And bring a cake. Chocolate, of course."

She liked to pretend Jerome was the chocolate addict. But really, she was ordering what she liked. As usual. But I didn't pick on her.

"Yes, Mother. I will be there." I hung up and tried not to think about it for the rest of the day.

JD showed up right after Mother's call. We nodded our hellos, then worked on the manuscript until my eyes blurred.

When I begged for a break, JD shrugged. We'd made progress, so he couldn't complain too much. I got up, stretched, and stumbled over to the window. There was a little bit of snow on the ground. Not more than a few inches, a dusting really, but it looked nice and clean. Like powdered sugar on an asphalt donut.

JD joined me at the window. He immediately checked out Debbie's place. What a perv. Lucky for me, her curtains were drawn.

"Good work today. You're not a bad worker, for a booze hound," JD complimented. I guess it was a compliment. "We're moving along quite nicely."

We were moving along, all right. We were, in fact, more than a hundred pages in. He'd been right about the control thing. Once I let go and let him dictate, he was able to work through me. It wasn't easy. It took a certain psychological restraint, but our speed was phenomenal.

Without looking at me, he asked, "Am I invited to Mother's for dinner?"

I started to laugh, but his expression was totally serious. Being dead must be a lonely business. Although, maybe not. I mean, what do I know about it? He could've had a swinging social life whenever we weren't hunched over my desk. Who the hell knows? Not me.

"Right," I said. "Like Mother wants a visit tonight, of all nights, from a stranger. A dead stranger."

He clucked. "That was a crumby thing to say."

I shrugged. "Look at it as a kindness. Believe me, you do not want to join me. Not tonight. Besides, haven't we had enough of one another for today?"

He gave me that puppy dog look. I couldn't believe it. Even dead guys resorted to this pathetic ploy. But it didn't work on me.

I headed for the shower, and when I came out again, he was gone, to wherever it was he went when we weren't together. In a way, I envied him his freedom. Especially his freedom to escape the special torture of family life.

As I gathered up my jacket and purse, I readied myself psychologically for a visit to my family home. Shit. My face was tight with anticipation. My crow's feet were turning into flocks, I was sure of it. The walk would help, though, smoothing that jagged knife edge in my psyche that popped up whenever I had to spend time with Mother.

Pain de Famille mainly sells whole grain breads, but they have a vegan menu, too. I'd heard they had some pretty good desserts. This was organic, healthy shit. The kind of food I usually avoided in favor of prepackaged junk. I lived on convenience. If it wasn't ready to eat in sixty seconds, I couldn't be bothered. But for Jerome's birthday, I would need something good and good for you. That's the kind of thing Jerome liked. And it was his birthday.

The snow had diminished already, the air cold. Too cold. I walked the eight blocks up Fifth to *Pain* to pick out a cake. If I was going to be late for dinner I could pretend it was Jerome's fault.

Don't get the wrong idea. I loved my brother. But he was family. And my family was madly dysfunctional. They really got on my nerves.

The line at the take-out counter was long, everybody ordering take-home dinners, loading up on soy-cheese quiche and veggie salads with arugula and walnuts. You never saw so many skinny rich bitches. Like ten of them, all in a row. Recovering anorexics on a health food binge? Sure looked like it to my savvy eye. The hungry, angry look on their chiseled, too thin faces reminded me of things I didn't want to think about.

By the time I got to the front of the line, the clerk was crazed. A solid woman with muscular biceps, she looked like she'd been on the equipment at Equinox or something. Sweat dripped from her nose. She wiped it away with one tattooed hand.

"Next," she said in the bored voice I often found myself employing in my similarly menial position at the Brewdha.

"What's your best chocolate cake?" I asked.

She looked startled. "Real chocolate? We don't sell

anything made with real chocolate. We only use carob. No sugar, either. Agave, other natural sweeteners." Her unfriendly eyes drifted over my head to check the length of the line. "Should I take the next person's order?"

"Is that cake carob?" I pointed to a round one with dark frosting. I didn't give a shit, but Mother would. She'd specifically said chocolate. But she'd also said seven o'clock. It was after six, and I was about to hoof it all the way to the Upper West Side. The walk would take me at least an hour.

My parents' brownstone was a prime piece of real estate situated in just the right neighborhood on West 87th Street. Nice, right? How do you think I afforded my little Midtown dumpette? Not on Big Brewdha tips. My parents had dough. Sad to say, they'd been helping me out. People my age, we have a hard time making it on our own. Take my brother. An even bigger mooch than me, he was still living at home. But I couldn't trash talk that, not really. Because every month, Mother sent me a check, a hefty donation toward the obscene amount of rent monies due. She'd drawn a line at my college loans, though. I was on my own with my outrageous but comparatively minor student debt.

I swallowed hard when the clerk rang up my purchase. Seventy-eight dollars for a cake made without sugar or chocolate? What was it I was paying for? An extra day of life? I could have grabbed something a little cheaper from the bakery aisle at the Whole Foods in Columbus Circle, but the *Pain* cake was already boxed up. I shelled out the ransom and got out of there.

The cake box slammed into my leg nearly every other step, but I did enjoy walking uptown. Once I got going, the air felt good, crisp against my face. The sky had cleared and it was all lit up with the ever-present light pollution. In Central Park, powder puffs of pretty snow dotted the grass here and there. A lot of people were out and about, joggers and kids in hoodies, grinds in their office suits wandering around because they didn't feel like going home to their undersized apartments or their oversized families. I knew how they felt.

I liked to walk wherever I needed to go. Take in the sights, a bit of nature, maybe a full moon now and again. Do some people-watching while I got from here to there. Manhattan is absolutely excellent for the hyper lifestyle. And you won't get mugged. Ever since they cleaned up the city, nobody's into crime that much. The muggers have been shipped out. I guess to Connecticut and Philly. And the prisons upstate.

I still had the keys to my parents' place, so I let myself in the front door and brushed the slush off my cowboy boots. I took out my cell and called Mother from the lobby. She didn't like it when I barged in on her unannounced. Even if she knew I was coming. She was real touchy about stuff like that. I had to be careful not to piss her off. I was bound to get her angry before our evening was through, but I knew enough from a lifetime of experience that I might delay the inevitable a little with my best behavior.

Told you I was a procrastinator.

"You're late. Where are you?"

"Sorry, Mother. Super crowded at the bakery. I'm downstairs. Be up in a minute."

The reference to the cake might have tamed her ire, but it didn't seem to improve her mood. I sure as hell wasn't going to tell her it was carob. Maybe she wouldn't notice.

"You know how I feel about Jerome's birthday. The least you could do is be on time."

I was only half-listening on my way up the stairs to my parents' place. Their apartment takes up the entire second floor. Four bedrooms, which is a freaking palace in this city. Plus, they had shared use of a large basement. Which are not all that common in Manhattan. What a prize. Because who doesn't need extra storage space in Manhattan?

What I really wanted to do was head down there and visit Daddy. Ever since he sold off his taxi medallion—for big bucks, you wouldn't believe what those things were worth back then—he'd been spending all his time in the basement. Tinkering with his wacky inventions. But Mother was still on the other end of the phone line, scolding me for my thoughtlessness, my unforgivable tardiness. So I had to wait until later to see my father.

I don't want to go into all the boring details, I really don't. But I will tell you this. My mother was one crazy lady. You're probably thinking I'm just being a bitch. I know, I know, mothers in general are slightly insane. They go nuts when their kids are born or something. Good reason not to ever have kids, if one needed a good reason, which I didn't. But seriously, Mother was a real head case. My brother hid out in his bedroom, my dad down in the basement. You figure it out.

The door to the apartment was cracked open so I let myself in. As always, the living room was overheated and smelled like Detour, Paris, Mother's favorite perfume. I set the cake on the Italian marble breakfront and stripped off my jacket, scarf, sweater, and boots. All I had on was a wife-beater and skinny jeans, but I was still hot. The place was like a steam room.

The table in the formal dining room was set, formally, with full china and silver, crisp white linens. Set for two. My heart sank. A long, lousy meal with just me and Mother. And no booze to ease the pain. You didn't need to be a licensed psychic to see the signs were all bad.

I was about to duck down the hall to Jerome's bedroom when my mother called to me from the kitchen. "Wash your hands, please. Then set the cake on one of Grandma Jackie's silver trays. Take one out of the bottom drawer of the hutch." Her sigh was heavy, tortured. "I'm trying to do what I can to resuscitate the roast. It's all dried out. Sitting here for so long."

See what I mean about guilt trips?

When I came back from the prissy half-bath in the front hall, with its lilac-scented soaps that nobody ever used and the shiny floral wallpaper that screamed 1970s, Mother was seated at the head of the table. She looked awful. Haggard, unkempt, her hair graying, limp. Dressed in a peach robe and fluffy slippers, skin as pale as the see-through chiffon of her night clothes. Her eyes were red and raw, like she'd been crying. Which she probably had. Mother spent a lot of time crying.

"I told you to put the cake on a tray, Jacqueline."

She was the only one who still called me that. I'd given up trying to convince her to stop. I could never change my mother's mind about anything. Once she'd decided on something, that was it. My opinion on the matter was completely disregarded. Even if it was the matter of my own fucking name.

"I had to put the cake up myself. Whatever were you doing in there?"

A teeny joint from my stash was what I'd been doing. Something to get me through the next few hours.

"Sorry. I'm kind of wet from the walk over. Just trying to dry off a little."

A lie, of course. But so what? I'd learned how to lie from Mother. She was the queen of lies.

I sat down at the far end of the table. She was giving me the hairy eyeball, checking for flaws. Of course, she would find a great many things that were not to her liking. This had always been the case.

She started with my hairstyle, if you could call it that, and worked her way down.

"I don't see what you have against hairdressers. You need a trim, dear. Once it's below the chin, your hair is just impossible. All over the place. Looks awful, makes your face look like a fox's. Long and sharp."

She had poured herself a glass of red wine. None would be offered to me. I was a child, would always be a child. If only she knew how little her view of me mattered. Out in the real world, I could drink myself to death if I wanted.

Sometimes I wanted.

"What's wrong with your skin?" Now she'd moved on to my complexion, always a sore point with Mother. "You look like you've been ill, dear. Have you something against blusher? Foundation, too, can work wonders for that pasty look. Use it on your neck. Cover up the moles, the creases."

Ha. She should talk. But I said nothing in my own defense.

"You've gained weight since I saw you last. I can see it in your jawline." She tsked. "You don't want to get chins at your age. You'll never get rid of them."

Mother worshipped at the altar of the anorexic. Like so many women in the buildings uptown, the high-rises along Central Park. Chicks on zero diets bother me, if you want to know the truth. There's something zombie about them. Masked for death. Don't get me started.

Mother downed her vino. Her eyes picked over me, weeding though my faults, ripping them out at the roots. Another night in the McMaster Arms. Twenty minutes in and already I was crawling out of my imperfect skin.

She opened her mouth to take another bite out of my ego, but I cut off the critique. Before we got started on my clothes, hips, ankles, shoes. My lifestyle, boyfriend, job, and lack of direction. All that would come up eventually. It always did.

I set down my water glass. "I'm not hungry, Mother. I'm going to Jerome's room."

She gave me the hard-boiled stare she used whenever she stopped pretending she cared. "He's twenty-two today. Twenty-two! Can you believe that?"

I nodded, my face impartial.

So? We all get older, right? Children age, too. No big deal. Get over it, Mother.

"Such a lovely boy. And so smart. A curious mind, right from the start. Always wondering about everything, figuring everything out. How things worked, how people thought. Even as a child, his

48

intellect astounded. Nobody had to punish Jerome to get him to sit still, read his books."

Yeah, yeah, yeah. Jerome was the brilliant son, Jacqueline just a hyper pain in the ass. We all knew the score. Jerome was every parent's prize kid, Mother's obvious favorite. Jacy, a poor second place, a distant runner-up. A disappointment.

Whatever. I stood up, on the edge of escape, but Mother snapped out of her reverie "You can bring in the roast and the red potatoes. If you want salad, there's mixed greens in a bag in the fridge. And bring in the bottle of Cabernet, will you?"

I was a good little doggie and went to fetch everything she'd demanded. But as soon as I was alone in her spotless kitchen, I poured myself a nice big plastic cup of California red, circa 2008. And drank half of it in a single gulp. Then I refilled the cup and tucked it away in the cabinet above the stove.

The cold stove.

I felt the smooth white surface. Cold as the porcelain sink nearby.

She'd had the food delivered. Why was I surprised? She rarely cooked. Why spend time in the kitchen when the phone was so much easier? Invite someone for dinner, plan a birthday party, then order out. Why not? Mother was the lousiest excuse for a mother. Even when Jerome got sick, she never made him the food he liked. Even though she adored him, she still couldn't do the slightest thing to nurture him.

The roast sat in the pan it had not been cooked in, the potatoes in a cold pot. Food arranged like a set with props. Why was she faking it with me? I knew she didn't cook. I'd grown up on her take-out food.

I cut a few slices off the room-temperature roast, dished up two china plates of crusty smashed potatoes. I grabbed the wine and, using my waitress training, carried everything back into the dining room.

After I served her, Mother temporarily halted her harangue. For a few beautiful minutes, she was still, silent. Uncharacteristically silent. Instead of her usual incessant attack on my looks, my character, my lifestyle, instead of dissecting me, arguing, lunging with mean-spirited digs, she just sat there. Staring at nothing, sipping her wine.

We both pushed the bland food around our hand-painted plates. Twice, I ducked into the kitchen for sips from my to-go cup. Mother kept hitting it herself. She put a nice dent in the bottle before she finally spoke.

"Cut me a slice of the chocolate cake, please, dear."

Chocolate cake.

As I reached for the cream and almond colored box from *Pain*, Mother gave me a spirited stare. Here we go. Round two.

"I wish you'd been more thoughtful, Jacqueline. You know Levain's has the best chocolate cake. Glaser's, they make a nice triple layer. Nothing like that cheap bakery outlet. *Pain* is a chain, Jacqueline. Imagine, a health food chain. Who ever heard of such a thing?" She rolled her wet red eyes.

If I said, "Yeah, and what about Chipotle? Those folks are mega-millionaires," she'd just snort in disgust. So I fetched a dessert plate and the cake knife and kept my righteous thoughts to myself.

After I cut her a fat wedge, I hurried off, not waiting to see her expression when she tasted what was sure to displease her. Back in the sparkling clean kitchen, the appliances as bright and shiny as the day they were installed, I sucked on my secret wine. Out the window over the sink, a flurry of light snow shook down from above. The scraggly bushes by the fence were speckled with white sparkles. The garbage bins wore shiny hats. Everything looked lightly salted.

I polished off what was left of my wine. Then I rinsed the cup and tossed it in the trash. On top of the greasy cardboard take-out containers from the Westside Market.

On my way down the hall to Jerome's room, I heard Mother sputter and begin coughing. I sped up, but not before she launched into full-out attack mode.

"What the hell are you trying to do to me now, Jacqueline? This cake is awful. I practically choked to death on it. Did I not say chocolate? Can you not do anything right? What the hell is wrong with you? Jacqueline?"

I didn't bother to knock on my brother's bedroom door. I opened it fast and slipped inside, closing it quickly behind me.

My brother looked up from his blue and white marble chessboard. The thing was a classic beauty, just like my handsome brother. His alabaster skin shone against his black turtleneck sweater, his teeth bright and even when he flashed me a grin.

"You really got her going tonight, eh?" Jerome snickered, his eyes sparkling.

Despite feeling henpecked and harassed, I had to smile. At least he understood. My brother could be a real pain in the ass, I guess like all brothers. But he provided an island of sanity in the rough ocean of

Mother. He could be counted on to take my side in most situations. Our twisted mother had always treated him better than she treated me, but still, it couldn't have been easy for him, either. She was such an insane bitch. I couldn't fathom how he'd remained at home all these years.

I checked out the board. My brother had a nice middle-game advantage against his opponent, who was failing to keep it together with a fucked-up Sicilian defense that would not hold much longer. My brother had two pawns all the way down the board on the verge of promotion.

I smirked, and Jerome said, "Do you believe this guy? In about three more moves, he's gonna get his ass mated."

The opponent was not in the room. My brother played old-fashioned correspondence chess against other serious chess players. Committed players from all over the world. They emailed one another their moves. The matches included many games and took months to complete. He also played online real-time games with high-rated players from around the globe.

Did I mention my brother's an international chess master? That's like significantly better than master, but not as good as grandmaster. A goal of Jerome's when he was younger was to play his way to the top. Grandmaster or bust. It's a tough road requiring a ton of international travel. At some point, Jerome dropped out. There's really no money in chess, unless you make it all the way and become one of a handful of world champions. In order to earn even a meager living, chess geniuses have to teach the game to attention-challenged elementary schoolers, something my brother was unwilling to do. He still spent his time studying chess rather than earning an income.

Like I said, moocher.

"Who you playing?" I asked Jerome. "Because he's a fucking fish."

He laughed a little, then scooted his chair over to a second small table with yet another chess set. This one was made from a smooth, highly polished, brown and white wood. I loved the soft sheen of the little squares, the Sugar Daddy and Vanilla Crème colors of the board.

"You're so smart," my brother taunted. "Let's you and me play a little blitz. I'll give you queen odds, how's that?"

I couldn't really play chess with my brother. Normal people couldn't. He was a pro. It would be like taking on Serena Williams in singles just to get a good workout. By the time Jerome turned eleven, he could beat me blindfolded, in minutes. I was a total fish, actually. But I loved sitting across the board from him. So I sat down and said, "You're on, sucker."

He set his chess clock for a five-minute game and we went at it, slapping those pieces all over the board. He beat me easily, of course, but I liked seeing him stop to think once or twice. Like I'd given him something to ponder.

When he asked if I wanted another round, I said sure. Anything to keep that happy smile on his face. "It's my birthday present to you, Jer. That, and the healthy carob cake Mother's all bitched up about."

He grinned. "Ha. No wonder she's been hollering. Carob?" He laughed.

We set up the pieces. They were old, leftovers from

his childhood days of rough-house chess. The black king's crown was chipped. One of the bishops was headless.

While he fiddled with the clock, he said, "You take her too seriously, Jacy. I told you, don't take the bait and never spar with her. You can never win with her. You know that."

I nodded. Of course, he was right. But whenever I was around her, I couldn't control how I felt. Like a sad child, an unloved one. And a loser. An angry loser.

"Sorry I haven't been around much lately," I told my brother before he hit the clock to start the next round. "It's not you. It's just—"

"No need to explain. I should get out more, come down your way. Meet you for a drink now and again." He looked at me. His pale green eyes were crystal clear, like he'd never done anything dark in his life. Maybe he hadn't. "But I'm just on the verge of mastering this new variation on one of my openings. It's fucking genius, Jacy. I could really take it to the next level with this one."

"You want to try it out on me?"

Of course, he'd crush me. I knew that, but it didn't make me feel bad. Never had. Jerome had always been better than me at everything, but he didn't rub it in. He was always nice about it, so nice that his irrefutable intellectual superiority didn't bother me. If you want to know the truth, it felt comfortable being the dumb sister. Except when Mother accused me of being the brainless kid in the family. I wasn't that stupid, just less than. I was always less brilliant than Jerome. Also, I was less controlled.

"Give me queen-knight odds?" I suggested.

He agreed, then proceeded to trash me in less than two minutes. We played hard, grabbing and tossing pieces in the race against the clock. The chessmen were scattered around the floor at our feet. We were both laughing our asses off.

We'd just agreed to odds for what was sure to be another wild rout when the door opened and Mother scuffed in. She rarely ventured into Jerome's private space. I didn't know what to say, so I said nothing.

To my surprise, she sat down. Perched herself on the edge of Jerome's tightly made twin bed, watching us.

My brother gave me a curious look that said, What the fuck does she want?

I made a little face, shrugged, and set up the pieces. Ignoring her, or trying to.

After a minute, she sighed heavily and said in a tiny, sad voice, "Jerome had no direction in life. I have to admit that to myself now, after all these years. He was a lost soul. Just like your father. Just like you."

My brother and I laughed. Give her a few drinks, and she'd talk about everyone in the past tense. Like she'd given up on all of us years ago. Just because she'd been born into a wealthy family and got to live like a pampered princess on a fat trust fund, she thought she had direction. Purpose. Some wondrous designated future, all set out for her. The rest of us were supposed to listen to her and do what she said. Get on track, stay on track. We didn't, so we were wrong. We veered off, made bad choices. We were drifters. And all drifters were, in her elitist opinion, lost.

Yet, there she was, sitting around all day in her smelly old bathrobe. That kind of lifestyle seemed pretty damn lost to me.

When I started to say something, Jerome kicked my shin under the table. Let her yak, he mouthed.

"Jerome's birthday is a difficult day for me," Mother continued in a semi-drunken monotone. "You know this, Jacqueline. You know how I struggle with my feelings about my son. My only son."

Jerome pointed at himself, rolled his eyes, and grinned like a goofball. He could make fun of Mother, and she wouldn't say a word. If I as much as sighed, she'd leap right on me. I kept silent, trying not to laugh at my brother's antics, examining the ragged edge on the head of the broken king.

"I know you think I'm a horrible mother. Because we've never seen eye to eye on anything. And you don't really respect my opinion. About anything." She looked directly at me, so I shrugged. She was right about that, no need for me to deny it. "But I do care about your welfare, dear. And it's clear to me that you're off your meds. You need to go back on your medication, Jacqueline. I don't want to have two children who, who..."

Jerome put a hand over his mouth to hold back a laugh. He got a big kick out of it whenever Mother tried to act parental, feigning concern about one or both of us. But I didn't think her commentary was in the least bit funny.

"You're the one who needs a checkup from the neck up, Mother. Not me. I'm doing great. I have a job, an apartment, a boyfriend."

Of course, she paid my rent. And that last bit was a lie, I was more or less between boyfriends, but so what? She didn't know the nature of my relationship with

Austin. Besides, last time I checked, I was indeed employed. Not gainfully, but employed nevertheless.

I glared at her. "I'm stable. You're the one eating dinner in a ten-year-old housedress from Lord & Taylor," I pointed out.

My brother gave a fist pump, but Mother simply exhaled. One of those, my daughter is a hopeless burden sighs. I kept quiet, hoping she'd just leave without any further slings or arrows.

When she finally stood up, her robe sort of slid back on her narrow shoulders. Then it fell open. I nearly gagged. Her petite body, which she'd dieted religiously for many years, was a horror. She was nothing but skin and ribs. Pale, saggy flesh draped across sharp bones. Like Silly Putty stretched across a pile of Pick-up Stix. If I hadn't covered my eyes with my hands, I'm sure I could have sat there counting those ribs. I don't want to even tell you about the way her pubis bone stuck out. Really, it's not the kind of image you want in your head. It'll depress you.

"Mother!" Jerome and I yelled at the same time.

She turned away slowly and scuffed out.

My brother and I burst out laughing. We made so much noise, cackling and hooting, practically weeping with disgusted hilarity, there was no way she didn't hear us.

Mean, right? We were being childish, I know. But who doesn't revert to juvenile behavior back in the family nest? I wasn't sorry I'd laughed at Mother. I wasn't sorry I'd come by, either.

We blitzed a little longer. He killed me a few more times, then I said, "Enough. This is slaughter."

Jerome laughed. "It was fun. I'll bring my travel

set when I come see you. I'll come by real soon." He was always saying that, but he never followed through.

When I hugged my brother goodbye, I said, "Don't forget about the cake I brought you."

He kissed me on the cheek. "Thanks, buddy. And by the bye, fuck her. I think you're doing great. I can't wait to read your new book."

I hadn't told him about JD, the project we were working on. My brother just assumed I was working on a novel. Another one, the same one, whatever. He was being nice. For some reason, he always seemed so upbeat about whatever I was writing. We'd fought a lot as kids, but as adults who still lived like kids, we were kinder to one another. I praised his chess. He encouraged my writing. Together, we kept our childhood dreams alive.

On my way down the hall, I checked my phone. I was already late for the date with Firth. But, since there were several messages from Austin, that meant I would blow off the nice guy who seemed to like me in favor of meaningless sex with a man who loved somebody else. Maybe Mother was right. Maybe my head was in a twist again.

My parents' apartment was deathly quiet. No music, no drone of a distant TV. Mother wasn't in the dining room. Maybe she was hiding in her silk-curtained, satin-pillowed bedroom, moping over the failure of those around her to live up to her bourgeois expectations. Whatever. A quick split would be best for both of us.

After I pulled on my jacket and boots, I ducked into the kitchen to see if I could snitch a bottle of something. That's when I noticed the carob cake. It looked like someone had taken a hammer to it and beaten it to death. The whole thing was smashed flat. Grandma's silver tray had a bunch of nasty dents in it. Ruined, just like my seventy-eight dollar cake.

I told you Mother was an insane bitch. Sometimes I hated that woman.

Chapter Five

I locked the front door behind me and jogged down the marble staircase to the lobby. That's when I remembered I'd wanted to drop in on Daddy. The basement door was unlocked, which was lucky because I didn't have a key. And if I knocked and called out for Daddy, I doubted he would hear me. My father could really bury himself in his work. He completely tuned out the rest of the world whenever he was busy with one of his inventions. His focus was intense. Jerome was exactly the same way with his chess study.

Fluorescent track lights enabled me to sort of see my way down the dingy cement staircase. The cellar was drafty, damp and cold. When I reached the bottom of the staircase, I held myself in a tight hug. Brrrrr.

My father sat at his workbench in a far corner, hunched over what looked like a miniature gas stove. His back was to me.

"Daddy?" My voice echoed in the vast, gloomy room. There were six apartments in my parents' building. The other tenants used the basement for storage. Only my dad hung out there.

I had to weave my way around discarded couches, leaning ten-speed bicycles, and stacks of cardboard boxes. I had to duck in order to ease past a long line-up of fake Christmas trees, careful not to get poked by the sharp plastic branches. When I stood right over him, blocking his light, that's when Daddy finally looked up at me.

"Babycakes!" He sprang to his feet and gave me a hard hug. A real bone cruncher. My father had always exhibited an ultra-masculine aura of suppressed violence. But in reality, he was a sweetheart, a soft touch. "What the hell you doin' here, darlin'?"

His grip was tight as ever, but his hands felt compacted, somehow. Like he'd lost mass, his flesh replaced by sinew and bone. My father was a small man, actually. A few inches shorter than me, his build had always been steely but slim. Now he felt almost slight. He'd grown up rough, stayed pretty tough. Rugged, the kind of guy you don't mess with when he tells you to get the hell out of his cab. A scrapper, that's the kind of man he was. Or had been for most of his life. But he wasn't getting any younger, and aging tends to gnaw us into smaller versions of ourselves.

When he let go of me, I said, "I'm here for Jerome's birthday."

My father sat down and shook his head, as if to clear it. "I'll have to run over to Levain's and pick up a cake," he said. "What the hell time is it?"

I needed to change the subject. My father could beat himself up pretty bad over his mistakes. Especially when it came to his relationship with Jerome. As many times as I'd reassured him he was the good cop, Mother the bad one, he still claimed he'd been the one to push my brother too much. Too hard, and too far.

"What's that smell?" I asked. "Are you cooking dinner down here?"

He laughed. "No, no. Your mother's meals aren't that bad. No, it's a little something I've been working on. A glaze. For chocolate bars."

Now I recognized the fragrance. Melted chocolate. But there was something else as well. Something sharp, acrid.

I peered into the small aluminum pot sitting on one of two burner coils. Something dark and creamy bubbled gently. I leaned in and took a good whiff. Immediately, I began to choke and cough.

"Please, baby. Stay back. I'm still working on this one."

"I guess," I managed between barks. Wow. That stuff had a kick to it.

"You aren't eating all this candy, are you, Daddy? It's not good for your heart. Not to mention your teeth." I pointed to dozens of chocolate bar wrappers strewn across his work bench. Hershey's, Godiva, Nestlé's. "It looks like Halloween down here."

My father smiled. "Don't worry, sweetheart. I'm not gonna die of heart disease. You know that." He pounded his chest and laughed again. "No, this here's for your dear mother. This glaze I'm developing will be a perfect addition to one of her candy bars. The last dessert, that's what I call it. Tasteless, odorless, and delicious as hell. See?"

I didn't, but I hugged him again. "Well, enjoy yourself, Daddy. I've got to run. I have a date."

"You're not still going around with that snotty fellow, the fuckhead attorney, are you?" When I nodded, he shook his head. "I don't like that one, Jacy. He reminds me of your mother's people. All fuckin' flash, no depth. No, no. I don't like that one."

I wasn't about to defend Austin. We were past that point. In fact, I agreed with my dad. Austin was a superficial douchebag. Still, I couldn't wait to wrap my legs around his waist and lick his lying eyes.

My dad glanced up at me, a kind of strange approval in his expression. He loved me, no matter how bad I fucked things up for myself. He reached over and gently patted my cheek. His hand smelled terrible. I coughed again.

"Babycakes, you do what you want to do. You're a clever kid. One of these days, you'll have it all figured out. You're going places, Jacy."

I held my breath when I leaned down to kiss him. Whatever product he was developing, it had a bad effect on me, scratching at my lungs. Daddy's cheek was stubbly, cold. Like smooching a coconut popsicle.

"You got enough money?" he asked. "You need some of last night's tips?"

Sometimes my poor father forgot just how long he'd been out of the driver's seat and down in the basement. I accepted a twenty toward my upcoming cab fare, then blew him a kiss when I got to the bottom of the stairs. He didn't see me do that, though. He was bent over his work again, stirring his glaze with what looked like a wire coat hanger.

I kept coughing all the way to Eighth Avenue. I didn't stop until I was in a yellow cab, headed for home.

****

On the way home, I texted Firth, said I was stuck up on 87th at the family funny farm. A lie, of course. I doubted he'd buy it. Oh well, easy come, easy go. Who knows, maybe he hadn't even made it to Collie's. Knowing my luck with men, he'd probably stood me up and would happily delete my text without reading it.

When I hurried inside my building, Austin was waiting for me. He was standing there in the lobby, in a sleek gray suit and bright blue tie, leaning against the row of little mailboxes. Like some ad for Hugo Boss. He gave me a nasty look when I walked in.

I was late. My big deal lawyer man was all pissy. Austin hated to wait around for anyone, especially a chick. I wondered how Shari was able to please him. Maybe she was one of those compulsively punctual people. Maybe the two of them were perfect for each other.

As it turns out, that was pretty much what Austin wanted to tell me. I should have known. Maybe I did know, but I was deep in denial world. I lived in denial world.

After I'd peeled off his wool suit jacket, unknotted his silk tie, stripped off his starchy shirt, and kissed my way down his rippling chest to the edge of his gold-plated belt buckle, Austin cleared his throat a few times. The heart-stopping sound of lawyerly disapproval. He should have been moaning by that time. I sure was.

But I can take a hint. Unlike some people. I stopped what I was doing and went out to the kitchen. The Stoli was calling to me. So I answered.

After a nice frosty hit, I said, "Okay, what's up? You angry because I'm late? I really don't think you have the right to—"

"Shari and I got engaged. I can't keep doing this. You know I want to, but I can't."

The freezer was open because I was about to put the vodka back. Instead, I slammed the door and hoisted the bottle to my trembling lips for another good slug.

"I'm sorry, babe. I'd keep it rolling, you know I would. But Shari, she's expecting."

I didn't want to know. Don't tell me. Don't.

Stupid me, I asked anyway. "Expecting what? Fidelity?"

That was a laugh. He was a prep-school brat, Ivy educated, a Manhattan solicitor. You couldn't expect anything more than devious frat boy antics from him. Even I knew that.

Austin rubbed his perfectly muscled, evenly tanned chest, massaging himself absentmindedly with his manicured hands. I wanted to leap across the room and suck his nipples. I should have been asking myself how he maintained his tan in the middle of winter. Tanning booths? How narcissistic could a guy be? But I was too caught up in the romantic tragedy of my life to see the reality of my lover. My deceitful, phony lover.

"We're expecting. Shari and me. The baby's due in late August." The fuck smiled when he said it. All proud, peacocky. If I'd had a gun, I would have shot his dick off. As it was, I went for a bread knife, and he had to wrestle it away from me.

I don't want to go into the whole story right now, though. To tell you the truth, I'm pretty embarrassed about it. We were lucky the cops weren't called. We were incredibly loud. A very ugly scene.

Yes, we did end up having sex afterward. Nothing like a long, hard round of I-hate-you goodbye sex, right? Austin made his usual happy animal sounds. I cried between orgasms. Before he could start snoring, though, I asked him to leave. I wasn't very nice about it, either.

"Don't call me when that stupid whore of yours is fat as a pig and just as ornery. Don't come to me for a mercy fuck when she drags your ass into hormone hell."

He laughed. But right after I said it, I realized that's exactly what had happened. First trimester morning sickness? Shari didn't want him to touch her? Who had he called for some TLC? The clueless fuck he'd kept on the side, that's who. His sorry-ass loser chick. *Moi.*

By the time he put his fancy suit back on, I'd gone from insane with anger to fully mortified. How could I have been so stupid? Shari was gorgeous, and dumb as she was, she worshipped Austin. Guys love hot bimbos who kiss their asses and mean it. Austin had never loved me. He'd just hung around for some of that from the one woman he knew wouldn't ask for anything more. What was wrong with me, anyway?

Sometimes I really fucking hated myself.

"Jacy, listen up. As an attorney, I feel it's my duty to warn you. It is against New York law for you to harass Shari. Please stay away from her. No stalking, no late-night calls, no threatening Facebook messages. No stealing her phone. None of that shit you pulled last year. Okay? I don't want to have to take out a restraining order. Please, let's not go through that again. Jesus."

"Fuck you, Austin," I said, but my voice was punky, small and weak. I didn't have the energy to go there. I really didn't.

"Okay, I'm going to have to trust you on this, Jacy. Remember, Shari's pregnant. You're a good person. You wouldn't want to do anything to hurt an innocent unborn child. My child."

"Fuck off, Austin," I said. "I've killed plenty of unborn babies. Just because this one's yours doesn't mean it deserves to live."

I was lying, of course. But my heart wasn't in it. He was right. Plus, I didn't really care about losing Austin. Once Shari came into his life, he wasn't mine anyway. Actually, he'd never been mine. Not really.

"We talked about this last year, Jacy. The meds were helping, you were doing really well for quite a while there. Maybe this would be a good time to see your shrink, go back on that stuff you were taking over the summer." He rolled up his four hundred dollar tie, tucked it into his jacket pocket. The way his hands caressed the smooth material of his suit made me want to throw up. "Just a suggestion. I know this is hard for you."

Was he smirking? The fuck!

"What part of fuck off don't you get, Aus? Just leave. Go. Now." I rolled over, giving him a last chance to ogle my bodacious butt. I know I have a terrific ass. Men have admired it openly and vocally. "I hate you, you phony prick," I mumbled into my pillow.

Was he laughing when he let himself out? I think he was. I swear to god, the prick was sniggering.

****

I didn't see JD all weekend, which turned out to be a well-deserved break for both of us. I worked two doubles, spending fifteen hours a day at the Big Brewdha. We were crazy busy. Microbreweries were really coming into their own in early 2010, if you remember. And we had some fantastic homemade ambers, a super strong dark reserve, and a long roster of fruit- and herb-flavored beers. Plus, we provided decent entertainment. Free. Self-styled bands, typically locals who needed a small-time venue.

All weekend long, my tips piled up, my feet ached, and my mind was on my tables, my orders, the menu, the kitchen, the bar, and little else. Here's the thing about waitressing. You have to really focus so you don't end up pissing off your customers.

Doubles were especially tough. After the first shift came to an end, I would already feel a mild but reassuring condescension. Most of the patrons I serviced were boobs, dopes, and useless dabblers, but they were my bread and butter. I could still crack a joke and a smile. The second shift, though, that's when I'd start to hate everybody. Every single person in the bar, everyone in Manhattan, all the sheeple in the world. *All* the sheeple. I really had to be careful or my badditude would show. Focus, focus, focus.

At some point over the weekend, I realized I'd never heard from Firth about our busted date. As expected. He was either oblivious, irritated at my flakiness, or he'd decided to forget about me. Whatever. And I heard nothing from Austin, which wasn't surprising, either. But to my complete amazement, I found I really didn't give a shit. I was depressed, sure. But I'd been depressed anyway. What difference did it make whether there was a man involved?

On Sunday night, I soaked my tired muscles in a hemp and shea butter bubble bath. I'd brought in all my candles, a glass of Pinot Noir, and a stupid gossip magazine. I was enjoying myself and, I realized, looking forward to getting back to work on the book project. If JD's predictions were correct, we'd finish the rough draft in a few weeks. Or less.

Next stop, fame and fortune. I sipped my wine and closed my eyes. Austin, schmaustin. I had a man who kept my future in mind. So what if he was dead?

Chapter Six

JD and I were taking a break by the window when my phone went off. Across the alley, Debbie was in the throws—and I do mean throws—of doggie sex with this really fat, astoundingly suburban-looking guy. I'd just about decided she was a pro, not some loose coed. JD agreed, but that didn't stop him from making a beeline to the window every time we took five.

I picked up the phone, turning away from the half-time show.

"I forgive you," an unfamiliar voice said. "But you have to make it up to me."

"Excuse me?" I was thinking about something else. Like whether I should heat up the leftover coffee. "I think you have the wrong number, bro."

"C'mon, Jacy. Let's not waste any more time. I want to see you again. And I'm pretty sure you want to see me."

Firth.

I wandered away from JD, who remained rooted before the window, mesmerized. For a big prude, he sure liked the live sex shows.

"Hey, awright," I said in my dumbest gangsta voice. "Whassup, man?"

Silence.

"Firth?" I asked. "You still there?"

No response. I glanced at the phone for a second.

Had I lost him? Usually the reception in my building was pretty solid.

"Hello? Firth? I think I'm losing you," I said.

"You will if you don't get on your knees and start begging."

I flashed on Debbie. Maybe he ought to be calling up my neighbor instead.

"You definitely have the wrong number," I said and clicked off.

But Firth was no fool. He could take a licking and keep on ticking. As Daddy liked to say about himself, before he got so depressed he had to quit driving cab. When my phone buzzed again, I answered like this: "Okay, okay. Can we please start over, fer fuck's sake?"

He laughed. Did I tell you how much I liked Firth's laugh? A big man's laugh. I liked the way he pulled it up from deep in his gut, then rolled it out, slowly, into a loud bass crescendo. Made me smile every time.

"A brilliant idea," he said. "And let's start with you inviting me over. For dinner."

Not a good idea. Not the way I cooked. "What about just meeting for drinks?"

But he'd have none of that. I couldn't blame him, either.

"No. Oh no, no, no. I don't want to sit at the bar at Collie's again, moping for hours while every shmuck in there laughs at my wilting bouquet. No, thanks. I want to arrive on your doorstep, right on time, knowing you're upstairs. Waiting for me."

Whoa. The night I'd stood him up, he'd brought flowers? For me? Guys never did that, not on a date with me. I wasn't the floral type. No flouncy gilt-wrapped boxes of chocolates, either. Maybe a package of lubricated Trojans. That was where my dates' romantic gestures usually wound up. On their own dicks.

I wanted Firth to bring me a romantic little bouquet of delicate flowers. I really did. So I caved.

"Okay, you asked for it. Dinner at my place. Any food allergies I should know about? Religion-based dietary laws? Health-related menu restrictions? Animal rights issues? Vegetarian, fruitarian, vegan? Ground nut, gluten, or lactose intolerance?"

Firth laughed, so I did, too. His laugh was absolutely contagious.

"Hey, my people hail from the highlands. Our basic food groups consist of beer, whisky, crisps, and hangover remedies. I come from a long line of doggie-style eaters. Put a bowl in front of me, step away. It will be clean in a matter of minutes."

"My kind of guest," I said, flashing on Debbie again. I glanced at JD, still rapt at the window. His monochrome face was unreadable.

"I'm an easy man to please, Jacy."

They all said that. In the beginning.

"You really shouldn't say that until you've survived one of my home-cooked surprises. I hesitate to refer to them as meals. Or dishes. Not until I see what they look like once I'm done with them." I wasn't kidding, either. My mother had not set a good example in the kitchen, and I'd never developed a flair for the culinary arts. "This little enterprise could pose a threat."

"I'm a pretty hearty guy. I'm sure I'll be able to take whatever you dish out."

That showed how little he knew about me. "You're

a brave man, Firth. A Celtic warrior. I admire that in a dinner victim."

I told him my address, and we agreed on Friday night at eight. When I hung up, I must have been grinning. JD tore his eyes off my neighbor's antics and gave me a quick onceover. He caught on right away.

"You like this guy. Firth, is it? What kind of a god-awful name is that?" he asked.

His attention wandered back across the alley. Every once in a while, a faint expression of confusion would mar his serene face. He had that what the hell look now, even as he carried on a conversation with me.

"Never mind, Jacy. Doesn't matter. The lawyer, he had to go. There was too little material for you to work with. He was just too insubstantial. All those Ivy League bastards are swells. They're so full of their own special fart-air. This new fellow, though. He's a big dope. Acts like he just won the Irish Sweepstakes. But at least you have something to work with. He's got some heft."

"He's a Scot," I said, but JD ignored me. He shook his head one last time at Debbie and her guy, at whatever they were up to, and headed for the desk. Our break was up.

Wait just a minute. I stood there like a clown, mouth hanging open. What JD had said bothered me. Not the big dope part or the Irish slam. Something else. I couldn't pin it down. His casual input on my boyfriends—how had he formed such strong opinions on my personal life?

Then I started to get a creepy feeling, a kind of buffeting paranoia. *The Twilight Zone* theme song began to play in my head.

"You weren't watching us that night at Collie's, were you?" My face grew hot. I'm sure I was blushing. "I mean, you weren't there later on, in Firth's apartment?"

He didn't answer.

Fuck! The guy was such a voyeur. I should have known. How could he resist spying on me? He ogled Debbie whenever he could. Of course he would keep a close eye on my sex life, too.

"Have you been here when Austin and I were…you know?" I sputtered.

JD rearranged his chair, sliding it closer to the desk, then moving it back. He kept his back to me, his head down. "Let it go, Jacy. We have work to do. I want to get through the end of the chapter, and it's already after three."

But I couldn't let it go. I felt it keenly. I'd been monitored, scrutinized in my most private moments. And judged. By a ghostly observer, whose dark eyes watched over me. Coldly appraising me as I made furious, spastic, drunken love to two different men. One my ex, a man in love with someone else. The other a total stranger on a night so fucked up I couldn't even remember taking my clothes off. JD probably remembered more than I did about that night at Firth's. I pictured his pallid, nosy face, the confused look as he saw me…whatever.

The blood pulsed in my head. I felt nauseous.

"Jacy, I will say this once, and then we need to get to work."

He was still messing with his chair and didn't turn around, so I moved toward him to hear whatever it was he had to say. Old coffee sloshed up my esophagus, so I swallowed hard.

"You are providing me with more than just your typing skills, you know. More than your writing skills, too, your channeling abilities, as it were. In addition to your physical assistance, your very necessary three-dimensional presence, I am relying on your youth. I desperately need your youthful input. Your spirit of adventure. Your past and present, shall we say, experience."

Whatever that meant. What about his dirty old man surveillance behavior? I wanted to talk about his peeping tom bullshit. I scowled, but he still wasn't looking at me.

He sighed heavily and sat down. "Listen to me, child. I'm counting on you to supply realistic details from certain aspects of your own personal history. I will need you to use these to flesh out some of the chapters. Because, as we both know, there are two vital thematic elements of popular contemporary fiction in which my writing is woefully lacking." He still refused to meet my eyes. "I am speaking of course about uninhibited sex. And mindless, impassioned violence." Finally, he looked up at me.

What was I supposed to say to that? I plopped down next to him. He was right. His story would need sex and violence in order to grab an audience, and that wasn't his forte. It wasn't mine either, though.

"It is indeed your forte, kid," he insisted. "More than you admit to yourself. But right now, we have work to do. We can talk about all this later on, once the rough draft's done. Now, let's pick up where we left off."

He leaned over and, with a speedy peck of one long

bony index finger, woke up my sleeping computer. Somehow, I was able to switch off the thinking part of my brain and get to work.

****

The week passed quickly and productively. The words streamed through me, and I let them. I stayed out of the way, typing furiously. It was like I was the ghost and JD was sitting in my office chair at my computer. Like he was writing with my mind, my hands, my body. We had merged. Yes indeed, to quote my favorite ghost writer. Somehow, the two of us had converged so that together we were bringing his story into this dimension.

By Friday afternoon, we'd completed a rough first draft. However, I still had surprisingly little conscious knowledge of the plot and premise of JD's novel. Because the way we worked was this—while I took down his ghostly dictation, typing as fast as my fingers would go, my conscious mind paid no attention to the story as a whole. Everything JD said flowed right through me. I listened for the individual words, sifting through them like a bag of marbles, picking out the shiniest cat's eyes, the prettiest glass balls. And then I scattered them, let them roll about. For all I knew, the manuscript could have been abstract marbles expressionism. It might have made no sense at all.

I did know this. The writing itself was exceptional. And natural. JD provided me with such a captivating, natural voice. But I was worried about whether this would be enough. Would JD's genius, his extraordinary literary style, his unique voice, be enough to get us an agent, a publisher, and some appreciative eyes on the page? Would his newest seminal work prove to be all it took to make my own literary dreams come true?

Who knew? Besides, first drafts were shit. We still had a hell of a long way to go.

In the meantime, I had a dinner to throw together. And relatively little time in which to accomplish this unpleasant task. JD took off for dimensions unknown when I headed out the door to pick up some grocery items.

Boy oh boy, as JD would say. Nothing like a domestic chore to make me lose my cool. Out of sheer desperation, I kept it simple and dropped into the Korean market on the corner for all the necessary supplies.

My menu consisted of the few dishes I was pretty sure not to burn, mangle, or otherwise fuck up. Asian chicken and egg stew. A dish that proved the chicken did come before the egg, at least when you followed this particular recipe. Garlic bread, with finely sliced garlic and real butter. All guys like warm bread with garlic butter and, let's face it, a one-armed monkey could prepare it. Steamed broccoli was out because the farty, sulfuric odor could overwhelm my little apartment. So I went with romaine lettuce and bottled dressing. Italian. Everybody likes Italian, right? I grabbed a couple of kiwis to slice up and top with a cute blob of vanilla yogurt, a sprinkle of cinnamon. I splurged on a six-pack of Guinness.

To my amazement, I didn't kill myself making the domestic preparations for Firth's visit. I mean I didn't vacuum, dust, or polish, god forbid. But I did whip up the meal, ferret away my clutter, and arrange the afghan over the sheets in a way that kind of resembled a bedspread on a made bed. And when I buzzed him in at eight o'clock, everything was ready and waiting.

Including me.

My date looked better than I'd remembered. He towered over me, beaming. He was at least six-three, with that boy-next-door face and a body to dream of. Totally sober and kinda nervous, I was wishing I'd grabbed a couple of shots of liquid courage beforehand. My voice shook a little when I invited him in.

"I brought you something, Jacy." He handed me two recycled brown bags from Whole Foods. One held a couple of bottles of wine. What would turn out to be a really juicy, full-bodied, organic red from Australia. The other bag mewed. Softly. "I hope you aren't allergic to cats."

Shit. Not one of those guys. Me and animal rescue people, we just didn't get along. I wasn't a rah-rah do-gooder, and it bothered me how most of those people behaved. Like they thought they had to let you know how much volunteer effort they'd been making. Not me. I had enough of my own shit to deal with.

It was all I could do not to roll my eyes and shudder.

Firth reached into the bag and pulled out a skinny black cat. With huge almond-shaped eyes the same green hue as Jerome's. Sea-foam green. The cat mumbled something unintelligible, and Firth cuddled it to his yummy chest. I wanted to change places with the cat. I almost purred.

"His name's Vixie. He's really a nice cat," Firth said.

Whatever. I wasn't really a cat person. But then the little critter peeked at me. His fur shone, and his bitty face was oddly, perfectly heart-shaped. I had to admit, he was a beauty. If I had to have a cat, if someone forced one on me, this was exactly what I'd want it to look like. Of course, I didn't say that to Firth.

"Is he a feral? One you've been feeding? I mean, where—"

"Vixie's my neighbor's. He had to go back to rehab, so he asked me to take the cat. You know my place—Alaskan outpost, like a fucken snow bank. Poor old Vixie wasn't having too much fun in my basement freezer. I just thought, I don't know. You're a writer, so... Don't all writers have cats sitting in their laps while they're working on their novels?"

When I laughed, the cat startled. He twisted around, jumped from Firth's arms. But he landed on his little white boots, his cute little feet. He dropped into place so lightly, with so much grace. Firth and I watched as Vixie sniffed around, sneaking down the hall to the living room. He tested the air with his wispy whiskers, curious, exploring.

Firth and I smiled at one another.

"He can stay here for a while, sure," I said. Why not? "He seems like he won't be much bother. Do I need to get a box or is he toilet trained?"

Firth grinned. His front teeth overlapped a little, but I liked the kiddie look it gave him. "I can get you set up with that kind of thing," he offered. "I've got his litter box, litter, collar. Back at my place. I'll bring over some cat food, too. So you won't have to spend any money taking care of him. It'll be like foster care."

I took Firth's heavy wool coat and hung it in the closet. While my back was to him, he wrapped his arms around me and hugged me. I closed my eyes, enjoying the sweeping warmth of his body.

"Hi. Nice to see you again. You smell great," he

whispered in my ear, his breath beery. He must have needed a little liquid courage himself.

Either he was a well-versed player who knew exactly what most women want or he meant it. I wasn't sure. There had been so many cads before him. And I wasn't like most women. A kitty and a compliment wouldn't melt my icicle heart. But he was charming and I was more than willing to be charmed.

Vixie disappeared into my bedroom while we were eating dinner. Which, by the way, came out really well. You can't go wrong with a simpleton menu like that one. Firth had three slices of garlic bread, a heap of salad, and two helpings of stew. He licked the plate clean, too, just as he'd promised. I wanted him to lick me clean. But first, another glass of the delicious Shiraz.

We'd talked about Firth, mostly. His family, his work, the college years that brought him to the city. He was from Vermont, a state I'd never been to in my sorry life.

"That's like living next door to a peepshow and never going in," he joked when I told him I rarely left the city. "Vermont is the sexy neighbor everyone admires but doesn't bother to touch. I love it there for exactly that reason. Not a lot of people, just millions of acres of rich green land. Pristine mountains, clean snow." He sighed. "I miss it. Miss my family."

His father and mother had immigrated from Scotland to run a dairy farm just south of the Canadian border. Firth was close to them, as well as to his six siblings and a pile of second generation cousins. So what was he doing here, four hours away from his loved ones?

"Vermont has its poor, the drug abusers, the troubled kids. But the real work is here, in New York," he explained.

Social work was demanding but rewarding, he told me. So sad to see how at-risk kids were mistreated at home, in court, in detention centers. So frustrating to understand the issues, how the parents needed jobs, stability, rehab, mental health care. But then he brightened when he talked about a kid he'd worked with who moved out of a crack house into foster care, studied hard in a new school, and got accepted to NYU. And another one, a teenage runaway who quit the streets and found a good job after attending beauty school.

"She cut my hair last week. Pretty nice, right?" he said, fluffing his carroty locks.

"Nice is right," I said. And I meant it. I was dying to sniff his colorful hair, run my hands though the shiny smoothness. His head was like a new penny, and I wanted to rub his bright scalp for luck.

I was enjoying myself. I really was. Firth was an easy conversationalist and a terrific storyteller. But when the chatter turned away from my guest's entertaining life and settled on my fucked-up family, that's when the night began to sour.

I shouldn't have had that third glass of Shiraz. Once Firth finished his stew, I should have stood up and offered myself for dessert. That's what I felt like doing. He was just so delicious. All I wanted was to serve myself a huge helping of Firth, lick him from top to bottom. I could have just started unbuttoning my black sweater, unzipping my black jeans. I'm sure the evening would have turned out better if I'd just done that.

Hindsight, you gotta love it.

"When you visited your mother the other night? How'd that go?"

He wiped his lips on a paper napkin. I wanted him to swipe that wet mouth of his all over my naked skin. Instead, I shrugged. I took another slug of wine and swallowed hard. My family as a topic of conversation was a turn-off. Major turn-off.

Vixie reappeared and began rubbing against my legs under the table. I bent over to pet him, mostly to escape Firth's gaze. Could he drop this detestable line of questioning and maybe get back to how great I smelled?

"From what you told me about your family, it had to be difficult for you. To go over there. And, well, sit with your mom. Even though—"

"Firth, my man," I said, my head tucked firmly under the kitchen table.

Vixie was purring. Already the poor cat loved me. And there'd been no deep discussions about where I came from, how screwed up it all was. Cats knew how to live. I was considering whether I might go nestle myself on Firth's lap and try to move the procession in a more animal direction.

"My family is not proper dinner table discussion." I sat up and gave him a plastic smile. "How about some sliced kiwi?"

"Sorry. But the night I met you, you were telling me all that stuff about your brother. And your dad. So I guess when you texted me about being at your mom's, well, I just thought—"

I slapped the kitchen table so hard the poor old

thing tottered on its skinny legs. Nobody should make a table with only three legs. Certainly not one people were expected to dine on.

Vixie skittered across the room and darted into the bathroom. But Firth didn't even flinch. He folded his arms across his chest and stared at me. He wasn't in the least bit fazed.

Typical social worker. My bad behavior was all in a day's work for him.

"Look," I said. "Can we please talk about something else? Anything else? Like, are you a reader? Do you read fiction? Who's your favorite author? Have you read *Chronic City* yet?"

He shook his head.

"No, you haven't read Lethem's new novel? Or no, you aren't a reader?" I was giving him shit, and I really didn't want to. I wanted to take his warm paw and slide it down the front of my jeans, that's what I wanted to do. So why was I being such a bitch?

"Jacy. The food was great. Excellent. My favorite beer, too. Not really. I prefer the heavy ales, but you can never find them. Anyway, enjoyed talking to you. Really like your apartment. Kind of utilitarian, the whole black and white thing. Not a bit fancy. But comfy. I can see spending a lot of time here. With you."

Who asked you to, was what I thought. The bitch part of me again.

"But if we can't get close, if we can't confide in one another, well, I should just leave. Now." He raised his bushy auburn brows, as if to say, "You know exactly what I'm talking about here."

And I did. I knew he was right. But I also knew I wasn't capable of being the person he thought I could be. Still, I didn't dare avert my eyes. He kind of had me. We locked gazes. I could feel the flush creeping up my neck.

"You were so open with me that night at Collie's. You showed me who you were. No mindfucks, no bullshit, no teasing. No frigging posing, none of the girlie shit I can't stand. No fake happy, no silly seduction games. I felt like I knew you, Jacy. Like we could get down to it, you and me."

I remembered so little, it was embarrassing. I couldn't even recall how we started talking, never mind what we'd gotten down to that night. I didn't dare ask him what it was I'd done to impress him. I sure didn't dare tell him I'd forgotten whether we had sex.

"I know I don't have to say this to you, Jacy. We talked about it that night. But I've been around. I'm thirty-three years old, and I've had my share of women and wildlife. I'm done with meaningless encounters, is what I'm saying. If I'm gonna spend time with a woman, I want it to mean something. I want it to be real. The Tao of Firth."

Corny. I could have laughed, he sounded so self-helpish. The New Age Goes Hallmark. But his face was serious, so I nodded. After all, he had a point. We weren't kids anymore, running around wasn't as fun as it used to be. In a high speed/high tech world of constant communication with people you never saw in the flesh, it had become increasingly difficult to relate to another human being. Life was largely anon. Meaning was in short supply.

Firth leaned forward until the table tipped precariously, then he sat back with a sigh. He'd been reaching for my hand. I hadn't been willing to meet him halfway.

"You want a man in your life, a person who cares for you? Then I'm your guy. You want to chitchat, gameplay and fuck around? There are plenty of other fish in the sea."

He was right, of course. There were plenty of fish in the sewer, too.

I stood up. I could have walked over to Firth and slid right into his lap. I could have taken his big, good-looking head in my hands and kissed him hard on his beery lips. But I didn't. I poured myself another glass of wine and said in my Big Brewdha voice, "The Australians make an amazing Shiraz. Your taste in red wine is excellent. Can I pour you a glass?"

I'll give him credit. Firth is a patient man. He put up with me, even though I was being my usual sorry-ass self. We even got into what I thought was an interesting discussion about the authors we liked and why. He was a nonfiction reader, but he'd liked Tom Wolfe's novels, too. That won me over. I almost forgave him for prying into my family history and scolding me for being superficial and aloof.

Almost.

When I asked Firth if he was a fan of *The Watcher in the Sky*, his eyes brightened. "My favorite book from high school," he said. "Best medicine ever invented for the alienated kid. I try to get the teenagers I work with to read it, but most of them can't. They just don't have the attention span, the study skills." He took a deep breath. "Because of what I see every day, I'm actually scared about the future of this country. Most of the young people I work with are never going to be able to make a decent life for themselves and their kids. They don't have any understanding of an inner life, of expanded consciousness, of psychic stability. They don't know how to make that happen for themselves. It's just survival of the fittest, street fight to street fight. They're like primitive animals in an asphalt jungle. Like aliens in an alienated world."

By that time, we were sitting together on the couch. The cat sprawled across my thighs, gray whiskers twitching in his sleep. Firth's body heat was inviting. More than inviting. I almost said, "That's me, too. I'm an alien in an alienated world."

But I didn't. When I yawned, he said, "It's getting late."

"Yeah," I agreed. "And I've got two double shifts this weekend."

He nodded his understanding, so I went to get his coat.

We hugged goodbye. He smelled like garlic, hops, and Christmas trees. I squeezed him tight, like I do when I hug my brother. But there was a distance there. I could tell Firth was disappointed in me. He'd wanted to get to know me better. Instead, he'd discovered he knew me even less than he'd thought. Another few evenings with me, and he might realize there was nothing there. That I was just another virtual stranger.

As I climbed into bed, I wondered if Firth would ever call me again. A few minutes later, my phone vibrated. I had it next to me on the night stand. The cat, who was between my feet in a nice warm muff, jumped up and off the bed. I sat up and turned on the light.

A text from Firth, thanking me for dinner and reminding me he'd drop off cat supplies on Monday. Vixie and I would manage until then. I had canned tuna and plenty of paper towels to wipe up any messes.

Eventually, Vixie returned to my bed. We spent a pleasant night together and, in the morning, neither of us felt the need to make a quick split. On my way down Eighth Ave to the Brewdha, I thought about what a sweet cat he was. How easy he was to love. I wondered why I'd never had a cat before.

Then I remembered: Mother didn't like animals.

Chapter Seven

On Monday morning, I couldn't get out of bed. After two fifteen-hour days of serving home-style burgers and beers to schizoids, I needed the extra sleep.

The Big Brewdha Microbrewery is an absolute lunatic asylum on the weekends. What I mean is, if I put you a rowdy room full of loud people with access to oversize glasses of freshly brewed beer, you'd probably go bonkers, too. Even the normal looking ones get crazy. The old folks in jaunty berets, the professors in their rumpled tweeds, the wallflower types in modest prints—set them up with a pint of high-alcohol reserve with hints of banana and pretty soon they're pink cheeked, laughing like hyenas, burping like madmen, and teasing the help.

Hey, I enjoy working in that kind of atmosphere, don't get me wrong. I can relate to the sense of psychological freedom you can get in a crowded bar. And when I'm on the receiving end of that kind of wacky joy, I get a contact high. Not to mention really fat tips. As long as I stay focused and don't go all hateful, it's all good.

But it's exhausting. It really is. So that's why I slept until eleven.

When I finally dragged myself out to the kitchen, JD was already annoyed with me. He sat stiffly in the living room, silent, simmering in his own snobby disapproval. I made myself a strong pot of Mexican dark roast, refusing to accept his guilty plea. Humming a Black-Eyed Peas tune and absolutely mangling it, I poured myself a mug of hot java and sat down next to him on the couch.

"Look. I was beat. Don't be like this. I'll make it up to you," I offered. Even though I didn't really owe him anything. "Don't you remember how it felt to work hard, then sleep late? I mean, it hasn't been that long since you croaked."

JD clucked. He stood up, walked across the room, scratching the back of his pale neck. Then, without looking at me, he fired me. What I mean is, he basically quit. How he expressed it was, he said he was done, and I'd have to complete the next phase of the project on my own.

"You won't need me," he said in this flat monotone, this almost dead-sounding voice. Then he perked up a bit. "It's time to switch from dictation to creation."

I said nothing. "Fuck you" was what I was thinking, though.

"Put that on my tombstone," he cracked.

He meant "fuck you." His little joke on the world that had banned him. Ha ha.

Okay, I got that he was annoyed and I was a fuckup. But why quit now? Just when things were going so well?

I huddled on the couch mainlining coffee while he paced around the room. He seemed so awkward. And distant, like he was trying to put space between us. He looked bad, worn out. Thinner and more whitewashed than usual if that were even possible. I could practically see through him.

"It's time, kiddo," he said. "This is all part of the process."

Yeah, right. I'd been dumped before. I knew the process inside and out. "Fine. Take a powder, then."

I thought about that for a minute. "Hey, where exactly are you going to go? While I'm slaving away on our book? I mean, am I supposed to revamp the whole thing in my own words? Without any input from you?" This seemed highly improbable, knowing his controlling personality. "Am I supposed to insert new sections, rewrite the story, edit it, expand it? In my voice? That's not what you want, is it?"

Vixie picked that moment to streak across the living room and leap onto the window sill. He liked to look out the window, just like JD. Yet another male voyeur in my life. Just what I needed. Vixie gazed into the alley. He flicked his skinny tail and licked his chops. I wondered what he was looking at, what he was thinking. Maybe he was wishing he could hunt mice in the street instead of licking tuna from a can. Or maybe he was watching over the feral cats, enjoying their freedom.

JD took up his usual post. "This cat is a real beaut. I swear to god, I couldn't have picked out a better animal if I'd selected one for you myself." He stroked Vixie's thick fur. The cat ignored him and continued to stare out the window. "Don't be afraid to trust your own voice, child. This is your challenge. I've given you the bones of the thing. Now you'll have to put some meat on it."

My heart sank. I could see my future, and it looked a lot like my past. The depressing past I wanted to forget. I was sure I wouldn't like what lay ahead. Without JD in the vinyl chair beside me, it would just be me and the empty page. Me sitting in front of my computer with nothing original to say. Long, lonely days filled only with me. Me struggling with me. Going head to head with me, myself, and my deep, depressing emptiness.

Ugh.

"Don't be such a sour puss," JD scolded, finally looking my way. His dark eyes were ringed, tired, and sad. "You won't be all alone. You have beautiful Vixie. And Firth's around. He's not going anywhere. He might actually decide he likes you. Who knows? Men can be pretty corny that way. Take my word."

He paused to see if I would respond. I shrugged. Whatever.

"And you can always go visit your lovely family if you need cheering up." He laughed.

"Ha ha," I said. "Very fucking funny." But it was good to see he had it in him still to tease me. Get a kick out of my discomfort. At least he didn't seem mad at me anymore.

"I am not in the least bit angry with you," JD said. "People who die, who leave you, are not doing it *to* you, Jacy."

When he walked toward me, the sunlight streamed through him. "Really, Jacy. Think of the untapped material you have up there on West 87th Street. Your genius brother. Your inventor father. The evil mother. Your dysfunctional relationship with all of them."

He made it sound like a cable show on Lifetime. "Then there's the history of mental illness. The violence. The substance abuse. The sleeping around.

The hallucinations, the blackouts. You have a wealth of material, kid. This is why I chose you. To modernize my work. To spice up the story. Make it hot, sizzling hot. You'll make it contemporary and that means marketable."

I opened my mouth but nothing came out. I really wanted to argue. To deny what he was saying about me, about what needed to be done, about the book itself. But sometimes you can't argue with yourself. You have to face yourself in the mirror and admit, yes indeed, that ugly looking reflection? It's you, all right.

I set my coffee down. "So I'm supposed to write about that stuff? My fucked-up family? Write about who I am and what I've been through?"

He gave me one of those looks. The grow up, kiddo expression he used when I was being especially dense.

"I can't do that." I got up to refill my coffee mug.

When I turned around again, he was gone.

****

Of course, I didn't do any work after that. How could I? Without JD around to browbeat and cajole me, my psychic energy was way too low. I didn't even bother to turn on the computer. I drank a lot of coffee, ate a couple of bowls of leftover kiwi with yogurt, played with the cat. Vixie loved it when you dangled something in front of him and then, when he got close, yanked it away. He'd keep coming back for more, even though he lost every time. Playing this little game with Vixie reminded me of my life—an endless series of almosts but not quites.

Who was I kidding? What almosts?

Two Guinnesses later, my phone rang. If I hadn't

been so bored, I never would've answered. That's the problem with boredom. It can really get you in trouble.

With a sigh, I said, "Hello, Mother."

"I need you to come home and deal with Mr. Ivanek. He's complaining about the basement again, and I have no idea what he's talking about." She paused long enough for me to roll a joint one handed. "Jacqueline?"

"I'm here," I said between little tokes.

"You're so quiet. What's wrong?"

"Nothing's wrong, Mother. You need me to come talk to your neighbor. Even though I was just there the other day. And you never mentioned it."

"He waylaid me in the lobby this morning. It's been months since he's complained about the basement, so I thought he was over it." She sighed. "Your brother's birthday. Twenty-two!" She sniffled. "If only I'd been a less excitable person. I think I might have been a good mother if my nerves had been stronger."

I dropped the joint and it rolled under the couch. "Did you just admit your mothering skills are lousy? Did I hear that right?"

I was down on my knees, but the floor under the couch was thick with dust bunnies. I couldn't see anything down there. I sneezed.

"Bless you, dear." She sniffled again. "I know I'm not perfect. I admit it. I was hard on you kids. I know that. But I did love the two of you. And your father. Even if I didn't always show it."

She loved us? Right. I could have started in on her about what kind of mother she'd really been, but I wasn't up for it. *What about Little Prince?* My brother's dog, the one she'd had killed, the evil bitch.

93

Just look, you selfish witch. Look what you did to Jerome. Daddy. Me. But I didn't get into all that because what I really needed was to hang up on her and locate the escaped doobie.

"I'll be over in a while," I told her. "I'll stop off at Mr. Ivanek's before I come up."

Before she could ask for anything else, I clicked off.

I was in no mood for West 87th Street. But at least now I had a plan, a purpose for the day. I could smoke the runaway joint, then push my way up Fifth, past the Gucci and Prada crowd to the park. Nothing like a long, cold stroll under leafless trees, under a cloudy winter sky, under the continual threat of heavy wet snow to underscore your suicidal gloom. Mix in a visit to the family funny farm, and you have the makings of a deep and deeply familiar depression.

But really, anything was better than hanging around the apartment, not writing.

****

By the time I reached the west side of the park, the streetlights were on. That's the kind of winter day it was, dark by four. The wall-to-wall clouds were sponges that soaked up the sunlight. It was frigid. My ears were kind of frozen, and my nose was running. I really could have used a hat with earflaps and a big bulky coat with one of those fur collars you can pull up around the lower half of your face. I know it's not politically correct to crave the skin of dead animals, but there was a reason our ancestors wrapped themselves in all sorts of hides. I should have been smart enough to do that, too.

I'd forgotten my gloves, so it was tricky trying to

unlock the front door with frozen fish sticks for fingers. Mr. Ivanek saw me fumbling around and took pity. He buzzed me in.

"What you doing out there in cold no hat?" He gave me a quick hug, a chuck under the chin. His raccoon eyes were as spunky as ever. "Below zero tonight. Brrrrr."

He mimed wrapping himself in a blanket, shivering, and I nodded. Mr. Ivanek is maybe ninety years old, but he's a nimble guy and his mind is still pretty sharp. He wouldn't walk around on a day like today dressed in a high school basketball jacket, baggy sweatpants, and holey sneakers.

"You see Mrs. M. now?" he asked me.

I nodded, and he rolled his eyes.

I followed his hunched form into the lobby. Mr. Ivanek reseated himself in one of the three velveteen wingback chairs that were supposed to serve as a visiting area. The antique chairs were the same ones that were there when I was a kid growing up in the apartment upstairs. Same snot green material, same tattered rattan backing.

Mr. Ivanek smiled. This was where he waited in the afternoons for the mail to come. I wondered if old friends of his wrote him letters from Bosnia or Croatia or Romania or wherever the hell he was from. He seemed to really get a kick out of picking up his mail. He'd been like that for as long as I could remember.

When I was a little kid, sometimes I would wait in the lobby with him. I'd sing him songs I learned in school, and we'd joke around while he waited for Kip, our postman. Once in a while, Kip would toss me a lemon lollypop. That's how long ago it was. No mailman would dare give candy to a kid these days. They'd get arrested for solicitation or pedophilia or something.

"How's Mrs. Ivanek?" I asked.

She was bedridden, according to Mother. The Ivaneks had a woman who came in every day to help. A nurse. Black, with one of those impossible accents, my mother had told me. If you don't speak the King's English with a Grey Poupon, boarding school brogue, Mother really didn't wish to speak to you. She wouldn't even try to understand you.

"Mrs. good, doing good. Your mother, not so good." He shook his head, waved his arms across his chest like he was umpiring an obvious out. "Basement. I tell her last time, no. No light on in basement. Lock up, no light on."

I wondered why he was blaming Mother for what was probably Daddy's carelessness. But when he looked up at me, I just nodded. I wasn't feeling so great. My feet were killing me. And my head was beginning to thaw out, pushing the blood all around. My ears were hot now, and they hurt like hell. And my vision was weird. I felt like I was shrinking, like pretty soon I'd be sitting on Mr. Ivanek's lap, waiting for Kip to spring up the front steps with our junk mail and stale lemon candy.

"I'll go down there and speak to Daddy right now," I told Mr. Ivanek. "I can remind him to shut the lights off and lock up when he's through with his work. Okay?"

Mr. Ivanek stared at me. He wore thick glasses with black plastic rims. His eyes were like soft brown egg yolks, runny and thin. "Daddy what?" he said.

"What you say?"

Maybe he wasn't so sharp anymore.

"I'll go down to the basement right now, Mr. Ivanek. Straighten everything out. Okay?"

He cocked his head at me. "No more key. Your mother has only key. No good."

I figured Daddy was the one with the key. Not Mother. She wasn't one for crawling around in dank, filthy basements.

"I'll make you a copy of their key, Mr. Ivanek. Drop it off for you."

He smiled. He liked that idea. Ninety years old, half-blind, and still, the man wanted to be in control. Territorial to the end. Oh yeah, that's another one of those traits that's got to be hard-wired in guys' brains. Like voyeurism. And fucking around with younger women, impregnating everybody all the time.

But I liked the idea of copying the key, too. Tomorrow, I could take Daddy's key to the hardware store, make a copy, and drop it off at Mr. Ivanek's place. This would give me something real to do. A productive use of my time. Yet another day's emptiness could be filled up, the void sealed with a plan. Running around. Errands. Activities. Busywork that didn't involve me sitting at my computer, enduring all the self-hatred that not working on JD's manuscript would entail.

I patted Mr. Ivanek on his frail shoulder and smiled at him. Then I left him sitting there while I hurried across the lobby to the basement stairwell. He was right. The lights were on, and the door was unlocked. I could smell Daddy's putrid glaze before I reached the bottom of the stairs.

"Hey, Daddy," I called out. "It's me again."

He wasn't at his work bench. And the little stove was gone.

I made my way around all the tenants' junk, trying to ignore the odor of rotten potatoes, the hollow coldness of the big damp room. I sneezed a few times, then coughed once or twice. When I got to my father's work area, my eyes teared up, stinging. Whatever concoction he'd been working with, it was majorly toxic. I held my hands up to my face and breathed into my palms, trying to screen out the toxins to prevent the acrid stink from entering my sinuses.

"Daddy?"

No answer. He wasn't around. He'd cleaned up all the candy wrappers, too. There was dust on the work table, and the tools were old and cruddy looking, caked with thick rust. A surge of pity welled up inside me. My poor father, hiding in the basement all these years. Just to keep away from her. My bitch mother.

That's when I noticed the candy bar. With the note on it. Swiss Milk Chocolate with Almonds, a yellow Post-it attached. Lying on the oil-stained cement under my dad's work bench. A gilt-wrapped candy bar, left there on the floor.

I bent over and picked it up.

J.C., Give this to your dear mother. Lurv, Daddy.

Lurv. He used to say that to me a lot when I was a little kid. He'd whip me up into his arms, whirl me about, tell me I was a "lurv." He'd never been able to protect me from her, though. From Mother. Scrappy as he was, he'd been cowed by her, too. Just like my brother and me. But Daddy had loved us. I was sure of that, at least.

I tucked the chocolate bar in my jacket pocket and went back upstairs. Before closing the door to the basement, I switched off the lights. Then I called my mother on my cell and told her I was on my way up.

Chapter Eight

Mother had unlocked the door and propped it open for me. I let myself in and closed it behind me. But I didn't bother to take my jacket off. I wasn't staying long.

"I'm here," I called out.

My parents' apartment is pretty spacious, so if she was down at the far end in her bedroom, she wouldn't hear me. I'd already warned her I was on my way up the stairs, so she couldn't give me too much shit about where was I and all that. Five seconds in my mother's house and already I was defensive as hell.

The hall floor gleamed. She'd shined it with lemon wax. I could smell it. My sneakers were sopping, but I didn't take them off. Let her piss her pants, I was in a mood. I sneezed like ten times before I got to Jerome's room.

My brother's door was wide open, which was highly unusual. He wasn't at the computer or either of his chess tables, which was even stranger. I stood there for a few seconds, staring into his bedroom, expecting him to pop out of the closet, a kooky grin on his face. But he didn't. The room looked freshly dusted and neatened. It smelled like furniture polish.

"What did the old goat say?"

I jumped. "Jesus, Mother. Do you have to sneak around like that? You scared the shit out of me."

"Language, Jacqueline. Please."

She was dressed this time, but not like a normal person. Her beige wool slacks were from the Carter era, the baggy cashmere sweater from one of her trips to Europe back when I was in high school. I wondered why my mother never shopped for clothes anymore. She'd been quite the shopaholic when I was growing up. Now she looked like she didn't care. In fact, Mother dressed sort of like me, like a hungover slob with a bad case of nostalgia and a Goodwill budget.

"Did you figure out what he wants from me? That man will drive me batty. I haven't been down in that basement for decades, yet the idiot keeps pestering me about it."

"He needs a copy of the key, Mother. He doesn't have one. I told him you and Daddy do, and I'll make a copy for him." I gave her the stink eye. "He's perfectly intelligible. You should make an effort. He's a really nice man to talk to."

"Hmph. Yes, well, you have an ear for these foreign tongues. I don't." She pushed by me. "I may have a key to the basement in the breakfront. I'm not sure. Your father was in charge of that detail. Not me."

I followed her down the hall to the foyer. She moved slower than Mr. Ivanek. I wondered if she'd been drinking. I couldn't smell it on her, but maybe she was into morning vodka. Bloody Marys. She sure moved like she was stiff.

"Where's Jerome?" I asked. She ignored me, opening and closing the drawers in the long antique dresser by the front door. "He at a chess tournament?"

Maybe he'd mastered the new opening and was back on the big quest to earn his next title.

"Please, Jacqueline. None of that nonsense today, all right? I don't think my nerves can take it."

Whatever. I started opening up drawers myself, clawing through dusty keepsakes and stacks of mildewed mail. Wooden chess pieces with cracks, ancient boards with rusted hinges. Broken Christmas ornaments. A leash with no clasp. Little Prince's royal blue collar.

"Your father never fixed a single thing he said he would," my mother said. But her voice had a nostalgic lilt, as if his ineptness were one of his best traits. "He was always gone. On the road, out at the airport, sitting in front of the Plaza. Out waiting for his damn fares."

Staying away from you, I thought.

I kept pawing through the junk drawers. Yellowing photographs with illegible writing on the back. Notebooks from various school years, mine and Jerome's. His were neat and well-organized; mine were messy, with sticker hearts and doodles all over them. I kind of laughed at that. There were stacks of colorful postcards with four-cent stamps. Coupons that expired in the 1980s. Crumpled contracts and warrantees. Bills. Lots and lots of bills.

"Jerome loved that stupid little dog." Mother was clutching the collar in one blue-veined hand, staring at it. Her hand shook like she had palsy or something. "I hated to tell him the news. He took it so hard."

The news? The *news?* The news was she'd had Little Prince put to sleep. After he'd pooped on her wax shine one too many times.

"You didn't have to take him to the vet. You could've given him away to somebody who didn't mind a little shit on their precious flooring."

"Language, please," she said, sighing. "You don't understand, dear. You never did. I had no choice."

"Right. No choice. Death to all who fail you, right?" I put my hand in my jacket pocket, fingering the smooth edge of my father's doctored candy bar. "You've won, Mother. We are all at your mercy now."

She tsked, returned the dog collar to the drawer it had been sitting in for more than a decade. "Don't be ridiculous, Jacqueline. Nobody has ever done a thing I wanted them to do. Least of all, you."

I laughed at that. Most of my life I'd done everything she'd wanted me to do. Until I finally rebelled, became a drunk and a wild fuckup. Which was relatively recently. Up until I went off course, though, I'd been the perfect daughter. The best sister. Neat in dress, mild in manner, clean in thought and deed. A diligent student, a hard worker, a believer, one of the sheeple. My use of language had been limited to an occasional, ladylike *damn*. And what good had all that being good stuff done me? None. Bleat, bleat.

"You killed Jerome's dog, Mother. He wanted you to leave Prince alone, but you couldn't. You wouldn't. You just had to ruin it for him. Like you do with everything we care about."

She tsked again and shook her head in disgust. After giving me the judgmental onceover, she said, "I do wish you'd go back on your medication. You're so angry all the time. This is exactly what happened last year. The anger about Daddy, about Jerome. You focus it all on me. It's upsetting, to say the least." She plucked a copper key out of a narrow drawer full of dirty coins and beat up plastic pens, rust-flecked screws and nails, rolls of tape and bent paperclips. "Is this it?"

I studied the messy letter on a miniscule masking tape label. Looked like a B. B for basement?

"I'll go down and test it out," I told her.

Maybe a little space between us would allow the tension to diffuse. I was ready to squeeze her scrawny neck. She never admitted to anything she'd done wrong, and she always acted so fucking superior whenever I showed the least bit of righteous indignation. We were right on the verge of an ugly shouting match. I didn't feel up to it. My throat was already sore from the little yelling I'd done.

I took my time going downstairs. Mr. Ivanek was no longer at his station. The day's mail must have arrived. I hoped he'd received lots of thick envelopes with crabby, foreign looking writing on the outside. Mysterious letters full of joyful news. Something well worth the wait.

The key fit. I locked up, then pocketed the key. As I climbed the stairs again, I fingered the candy bar. Why did Daddy want me to give the chocolate to Mother, anyway? What was on it? His secret recipe for the perfect candy coating? What kind of dessert glaze smelled like high school chemistry class? Could he have made her a toxic treat? One that could actually make her ill? Or even do her in?

How Hollywood!

I didn't think my father would poison his own wife, no matter how much of a nasty twat she'd been over the years. I just couldn't see it. So I doubted the candy would make her sick. But, on the other hand, I wouldn't have been totally shocked if it did. Really, who could blame the guy?

When I got back upstairs, Mother said, "You had

the key all along. I found it on your keychain. Why did you lie about it?"

I'd left my keys on the breakfront. But I didn't have the basement key. She was on a crazy rant.

"Don't be ridiculous, Mother."

I snatched the key from her hand and matched the two keys together, lining them up. Sure enough, they matched. She hissed at me.

So it was true. I had one of the missing keys. But so fucking what? "Look, Mother, calm down. What's the big deal? Now we have the key, two of them. So I'll drop one off at Mr. Ivanek's on my way out."

Of course, that wasn't good enough. She ragged on and on about how forgetful I was, how irresponsible. What a mess my life was. All the usual complaints.

"You look disheveled. You're confused. I'm worried about you. In fact, I think I should call your therapist." Her eyes popped, making her appear on the edge of bursting. "In fact, I think I will instruct the doctor to *make* you take your medication. Or..."

When she paused, I said, "Or what, Mother? Or you'll send me somewhere for a professional make-over?"

Like that would work. Fuck off, Mother.

If she hadn't been such a terrific bitch, I might not have left the chocolate bar on the kitchen counter. I might have taken it with me and dumped it when I got home. Just in case. Just in case Daddy'd gone mad. But all the squabbling left me feeling like I had no choice. She deserved whatever Daddy had in mind when he concocted his special glaze. So, I ducked into the kitchen and dropped off the candy bar. Right there, on the counter, next to the smashed up tray still dotted with carob crumbs.

I left her that toxic present. With my best unspoken wishes.

****

On my way down Eighth Ave, my phone vibrated.

"You're crying," Firth stated. He sounded totally nonjudgmental about it. Which I really fucking appreciated, boy. "Either that, or you have a bad cocaine habit you've forgotten to tell me about."

I sniffled, then sneezed.

"Oh, shit. You're allergic to Vixie. Damn. I'll come get him tonight as soon as—"

"Relax, friend," I said. "Vixie and I are doing great. I'm not even at my place. I'm on my way back there. From 87th Street."

"Oh ho," he said. "So this is your post-familial-visit voice. Aha. And what did she do to you this time?"

He sounded like he knew an awful lot more about me than he should have. "You mean Mother?" He didn't respond, so I said, "She had an issue with the basement. I'm taking care of it for her."

"The fucken basement. Were you down there? No wonder you're upset."

What exactly had I told him about my parents and their crappy basement, anyway? I didn't want to think about it, so I didn't. But one of these conversations, I would have to admit just how little I could recall from the night we'd met.

I waved at a passing cab. The weather had gone from cold to worse. My body shook, both from the icy wind and whatever was making me sick. The basement? The candy bar I'd left behind? My horror movie mother? My freaking life?

Firth silently waited for me to open up. I waited for the cab to pull over, then jogged to catch it.

Okay, okay, so my family was fucking toxic. Why was it so difficult for me to talk about this? Yeah, yeah, Firth and I, we needed to get into it. We'd obviously done it before and now we had to do it again. This wasn't the time, though.

It never felt like the time to talk about shit like this.

Remember I told you I met him at a bar, but I didn't want to go into the whole story? This was exactly the kind of thing I meant.

I yanked open the back door to the shiny yellow cab and hopped in. While I was telling the cabbie my address, I could hear Firth's soft breath on the other end of the line. Patient. Kind. Good, and good for me. He was a healthy choice, like something you could buy at *Pain de Famille*.

Still, I didn't want to go there. I really didn't. But if I wanted to have any kind of relationship with the man, I knew I'd have to. Eventually.

In the meantime, I could procrastinate.

When the cab eased into uptown traffic, I coughed and said, "Jeez, sorry," then coughed some more. I wasn't faking it, either.

"Maybe this isn't the time to discuss your family," my insightful friend concluded.

I relaxed against the seat between coughing jags. The cab blew canned heat in my face, and it felt so fucking warm and cozy I wanted to lean forward and kiss the cabbie's wrinkled raisin of a cheek.

"I'm bringing the kitty supplies over tonight, after practice. We'll talk then," Firth said.

I agreed, just to get rid of him. But Firth didn't

hang up. Instead, he lowered his voice and asked, "You going to be okay?" Like he cared.

"Sure, I'm fine." Wasn't I?

"How many Guinnies you got on hand?" he asked.

Once I figured out he meant bottles of Guinness, not foreign money or spare Italians, I said, "I still have one or two."

"Not nearly the right answer," he replied. "And from the sound of things, you're going to need some chicken soup with garlic, too. How's seven o'clock sound?"

It sounded excellent, and I told him so.

Chapter Nine

By the time Firth arrived, I was in pretty rough shape. Flu, or something a lot like it. My slitty eyes watered, I coughed whenever I tried to talk, and my head hurt like hell. He walked in with a six-pack of Guinness and a plastic quart container of hot soup.

My hero.

I dragged myself back to the couch and collapsed again while my guest messed around in the kitchen, looking for soup bowls, boiling water for tea.

I closed my eyes for a second, and when I opened them again, garlicky soup bubbled gently on the stove. Firth sat at the kitchen table with a paperback, sipping his creamy beer, Vixie curled in his lap. If I hadn't had the whirlies so bad, I would have thought we were the picture of domestic bliss.

"*Chronic City*? Good choice, my friend," I croaked.

"She speaks, Vix," Firth announced, and the cat yawned, languorous. "How you feeling? Can I interest you in a bowl of soup? It's really good for your respiratory system. Paetra, off Tenth down by my place? She makes the best stock. This little hole-in-the-wall Eastern European deli. I go by there whenever I think I'm coming down with something."

I reached up a hand and felt around. My hair was matted to one side of my head, a hard mass of drool dried on my cheek. I had to look like something the cat had coughed up. But Firth grinned at me. It was disorienting.

"You getting up?" he challenged.

When I struggled to my feet, Firth stood, too. The cat dropped to the floor, then slunk away to investigate his new furnishings.

I must have nodded off, because I sure hadn't seen Firth bring in all the cat supplies. When I looked around, I noticed my new roommate had settled in quite nicely. A litter box now enhanced the minimalist white-on-white décor of the bathroom, a battered scratch bar sat under the window in the living room, and a lovely set of aqua bowls were tucked into a corner on the kitchen floor. Bags of Pussy Cat Vitamin Diet had appeared in my pantry like magic. And a cat brush nestled right next to mine on the shellacked slice of tree trunk I used for an end table.

My guest pulled out a vinyl chair for me and indicated I should join him at the kitchen table. So I did. He served me a steaming bowl with some kind of really delicious, lightly salted rice crackers. I was surprised I had any appetite. Actually, once I started eating, I was ravenous. Feed a cold, starve a fever? Or was it the other way around? I never could get that straight.

Seated across from me, Firth watched as I wolfed food, swiped goo from my eyes, and coughed. What a turn on for him.

"Aren't you worried you'll catch this?" I managed to choke out between ragged breaths. "Miss work?"

"Nah. It's a risk I feel like taking. Besides, I like hanging out here. It's warm and it smells good. Me and

Vixie, we're happy here. Looks like you may have taken in two lonely critters. Don't think either of us will want to go home again after this."

I laughed. This made me hack. Firth reached into a shirt pocket and handed me a cough drop. "Mentholated eucalyptus. Works great."

He'd thought of everything. I wanted to curl up in his lap, now that Vixie had wandered off. I was pretty sure the man would have me purring in no time.

He washed out my bowl for me and set it in the rack to air dry. His back was so wide he seemed to overwhelm my little galley kitchen. As shaky as I was, I had to go for it. I walked over to the sink and wrapped my arms around his thick, taut waist. He reached back and held me tight against his big warm body. We stood like that, at the sink, for a long moment. My hot face on his plaid wool shirt, his strong hands gripping my hips.

"I wish I wasn't sick," I said into his scratchy shirt.

"We have all the time in the world. You'll be well soon enough."

Such a mature thing to say. I coughed a few more times, then went to bed.

Later, when my fever was really high, I wondered whether I might have imagined our romantic scene at the sink. The memory felt false or embellished. And the scene itself was one that normally would have turned me off. So cutesy and corny. Gag material, like a couple of goofy sweethearts in a two-hanky Hallmark movie.

It was real, though. Firth was the real deal.

****

The next day was pretty rough, with me feverish, dazed, too exhausted to get out of bed. I slept a lot, kept my phone off, and wallowed in the stillness of my apartment. The only sounds were my hoarsey coughs and the patter of Vixie's feet whenever he jumped down from the bed. Once I heard him scratching in his litter box. What a good boy.

That's why I freaked out when I awoke to the sounds of chatter and subdued laughter. The fuck? There were people out in the living room? *My* living room?

I froze, unable to move or breathe. Vixie lay on my chest. I could hear his soft, regular breaths. Beyond the open doorway, light spilled across the hall flooring. Somebody clinked glasses with somebody else. A dog barked.

When I tried to sit up, I couldn't move my limbs. I could barely lift my head. It was like I'd been flash frozen and I was thawing out, but slowly. Very slowly. If I hadn't been feverish, I might have been scared to death. Instead, the situation felt distant, dreamy. Hallucinogenic.

"She needs to go back on her meds," was the first thing I heard clearly enough to understand. "She thinks all this is real."

Someone got up from the couch, someone else plopped down on it. A dog skittered across the floor, then whined at the door. It probably wanted to go out.

"She looks like shit. I'm worried about her," someone said.

"Language, please."

Shit. I knew those voices. Mother. Daddy. Jerome. I listened to them talking about me. Somebody said Lexapro. Somebody else said Abilify. And Klonopin. I struggled with my rubbery body until, finally, I managed to sit up.

That's when I heard another voice say, "You people need to leave her alone. She's working right now." JD? Talking to my family? "Keep this in mind, writers are always half-crazed when they're working." My ghost spoke in a bossy tone I knew only too well. "It's par for the course."

That was a cliché, but it was nice of JD to defend me. Except I wasn't actually working. I wasn't doing much of anything. Procrastinating, mostly. Traipsing around the city on dumb errands. And now, lying around feeling awful.

Being sick is a terrific way to put off your life. Take my word.

When I could move my legs, I got out of bed. Vixie, however, didn't budge. He seemed to stay behind, not moving, in the same position on my chest. I was confused, not sure how that could happen, but I shook off the dichotomy of my reality and tiptoed over to the doorway.

The living room light jabbed at my eyes until I shaded them with my hands. I had to peek out through my fingers. My palms smelled like eucalyptus. I'd been gorging on the cough drops Firth had left behind.

"Jacqueline never could deal with the truth, Jerome." Mother tsked. "She's starting to lose ground again. We need to act quickly."

My knees gave out, and I slid to the floor and leaned against the wall. I was confused, dizzy, enthralled. My whole family had come to my apartment together out of concern for me? These were the things other people's loved ones did. Not us. Not my family. And certainly not in order to help *me*.

"You have no idea what I would have to go though. Those places cost an unimaginable amount of money." Mother sighed. I pictured her tired face, the deep frown lines, the ugly disappointment there.

Daddy piped up. "What about the medallion money? She could use that to pay for whatever treatment she needs. After all, that's why I sold that fucking thing. To provide for my lurv—"

"Language. Please!"

A long pause. The dog whined again. Whose dog had they brought to my apartment? I was surprised Vixie was oblivious to the canine presence.

"Come, come," JD interrupted. "Enough crapping about. We're all here tonight to discuss what can be done to help Jacy."

"If she hadn't slipped me the tainted chocolate, I might have been able to convince her to go back on her medication," Mother said. "As it is, my body's already cold. It's over for me. I'm a stiff. There's nothing I can do anymore. I can't change anything."

"That's where you're wrong," JD said. "Now is the best time. Finally, you can begin to influence your daughter's choices. While you were alive, she refused to listen. Now that you're dead, it will be a different story entirely."

Dead? *Dead?* What the hell was he talking about? If the chocolate had been poisoned, and she'd eaten it, how could Mother be here now, in my living room, with my father and brother? I didn't get it. How could the three of them converse with JD, who was, indeed, dead? A ghost available only to me, my semi-imaginary writing muse.

Or so I had thought. Because wasn't my ghost

writer just a part of my own mind?

Everything began to blur as my head, overloaded with conflicting information, fuzzed up. I couldn't focus, I was overwhelmed with a dazed numbness. I had questions I needed to ask, but I was in no shape to ask them. When I tried to stand up, my legs refused to cooperate. Wobbling, I slid down the wall again.

I let the wall hold me for a while.

"You folks don't get it," JD said. "The best way you can help her is to go away and leave her alone. As long as she has all of you in her head, telling her what to do and what to think, she's unable to make a healthy decision for herself." He paced, his shoes tapping back and forth across the floorboards. "I'm afraid I've been the same way. Another personal advisor, influencing her decisions, living through her and, in that way, not allowing her to live for herself." His pacing stopped. "She doesn't know this, but I'm out. Done. I'm not coming back. I'd suggest all of you do the same. This will be the best thing we could do for her."

The dog whined, then howled.

"Hush." Mother's voice sounded cool, distant. She was all ice when she wasn't feeling sorry for herself. "If we need to leave the girl alone, then we need to leave her alone. I think we should all agree to do this. We are family, and we should make a family pact."

I could hear them murmuring their ascent.

Those fucking weaklings! As usual, they'd been cowed into submission by that bossy bitch.

The dog let out a pitched yowl. The sound was ear piercing.

"Little Prince, stop that eternal whining!" Mother yelled.

Little Prince? My mind reeled.

"He doesn't like being in the same room with you, Mother. After you sent him to the gas chamber on that trumped up charge."

"Oh, Jerome. That was years ago. Can't you just forget about it?" Mother sighed in exasperation.

JD cut in with, "I propose we make a final toast to our agreement. Agreed?"

I heard them. They all agreed to cut me loose. Hip hip hooray, let's all abandon Jacy to her crumby life.

Then those fuckers clinked glasses. Were they drinking my wine? Invading my space, helping themselves to my life, only to decide they would dump me like so much unwanted baggage?

A burst of hot anger shot through me, revving me up enough that I rose to my feet. Steadying myself against the wall, I got my sea legs under me. Then I stumbled out into the light, eyes slitted, rage gushing from my sweaty pores.

The living room was empty. A stream of bright yellow painted the floor from the front window, trailing across the living area to the bedroom. The light was coming in from the halogen street lamps outside. I'd forgotten to pull the curtains.

Confused and weak, I stumbled back to bed. Vixie wasn't there, but at some point he reappeared, settled back down again on my chest.

****

In the morning, I wondered if the whole thing had been a fever dream. A weird, creepy sort of sickness vision. A nightmare caused by my high temperature.

I was feeling more like myself, so I stripped the bed. Then I made up the bed with a spare set of clean white sheets. I tidied the apartment and made coffee.

When I called my mother, she answered on the first ring. I didn't want to talk to her, though, so I hung up. Obviously, she hadn't been poisoned by Daddy's candy bar. I should have known right away the visit wasn't real. Mother would never arrange a family meeting to discuss my welfare.

After a hot shower, I went to the supermarket, then took a short walk around the block. The weather was unseasonably warm, the sky a faded denim blue. Whenever you get over an illness, life looks good. You know how wonderful it feels just to be out of bed, back out in the world? That's how I felt. For me, this kind of lightness of being was rare. And fleeting. I wallowed in it, firmly closing my mind to all the night's insane revelations from the family intervention dream.

I called Firth while I was still wandering the sweet-smelling streets, delirious with aliveness. Something was in bloom, and I could have sworn it was lilacs. As soon as he answered, I invited him to meet me at Joy Luck for dinner. I wanted to thank him for taking care of me. He suggested take-out instead. And he offered to pick up.

"League tag game tonight. City Ruggers versus the Holy Shits from Brooklyn. We'll beat those lads' fucken asses, but I don't know how long it'll take. I'll come over after. Be ready to chow down."

I said okay and we hung up. Another evening with Firth sounded terrific. I wandered into a flower shop and bought a couple of sunflowers from Mexico or somewhere. Then I went to my favorite café for a green chai tea to go.

The line was long, as usual, but I didn't mind

waiting. We'd be eating dinner late, so I had plenty of time and no excuses. I needed to sit down at the computer and, if nothing else, at least read over the draft JD and I had prepared. I wasn't in a hurry to begin, however. What if I discovered the manuscript totally sucked? What if the time I'd spent writing with JD had been one long fever dream?

Tea in one hand, flowers in the other, I stopped at the Korean market for a six of Guinness, which I tucked under my arm. Then I stood out front to watch the city flood past. So many beautiful faces from all over the world. Strong legs, trim bodies, expensive tailored clothing. The Asian women with their sleek black hair. Young men in pinstripes and brightly colored ties. Lovely girls in short skirts, long legs white as clouds in a soft spring sky. In this bustling city, I could people-watch all day. What went on in everyone else's head? Did dead people talk to them, too? Were we all haunted by our pasts, our unknown futures?

Of course, I knew what I was really up to, hanging around on the streets, enjoying my freedom, my newfound health. Yes indeed, I was simply doing what I did best. Avoiding reality. Procrastinating again. Delaying my impending return to face what my ghost writer, and I had begun. Here I was, casually not getting going on what I had to do. Which was to sit down and fucking deal with the incomplete manuscript.

Ugh.

Before I dragged myself home by the short hairs, I went for one more delay tactic. I'd been curious, so I checked out the alley between my building and Debbie's. I was looking for feral cats, the empty aluminum trays that indicate homeless critters were using the alley as a feeding station. But there was nothing. I wondered again what Vixie looked at while he sat at the window, transfixed, his tail occasionally flicking.

As I turned away, a large, florid woman with baggies on her feet scuttled out from behind one of the stinking dumpsters. In a sad croak of a voice, she asked me if I had any change. I gave her a couple bucks.

"Bless you and your screwball life," she said, stuffing the money down the front of her soiled sweater.

She seemed entirely sincere, so I thanked her. Yeah, my life was screwball all right, but there were days when I realized just how fortunate I was.

I'd finally run out of ways to not do what I had to do. I'd go home now and start with the manuscript. Sighing heavily, then deep-breathing the clear air, I lugged my goodies back to my building. It was time to head upstairs and say hello to the screen.

Vixie greeted me at the door, tail swishing. When I cracked open the living room window to allow in some of the day's freshness, he hopped up. I made more coffee, sucked it down, perking myself up until I was energized beyond all excuses. There would be no napping while I was reading the manuscript. JD's masterpiece. My masterpiece.

Vixie left his post to sit with me for the big event. He kneaded my lap while I opened the file, took a deep breath, and began reading.

At some point, the cat must have jumped down. I didn't notice that or anything else around me. By the time I closed the file, the room was dark and my stomach growled with hunger. The doorbell buzzed. As I stood up in a daze to answer the door, I realized the apartment was freezing cold. I had no idea what time it was.

What I did know was this—the novel was fantastic.

Yes, there was a ton of editing to do. Some cutting here and there, plot holes to fill, skimpy surfaces in need of further expansion. I wasn't at all sure where I'd add the sex scenes JD had said he wanted, never mind the violence he seemed to think I could simply insert somewhere in the text. But all that was of little concern because the manuscript was so near to perfection. Everything a story requires was already in there—gripping plot, interesting characters, conflict, suspense, humor. And the language! JD's new novel was an absolute tour de force.

The minute I opened the door, Firth leaned in to kiss my cheek. He was grinning. He had something in his hands, which he hid from me. "Hey, you're back from the dead. You look great, Jacy."

Dead?

I must have blanched because he said, "Really, honey. You look back to normal."

I knew that wasn't accurate, either. I couldn't possibly look normal. I didn't even look presentable. I hadn't changed out of my sweaty clothes, I hadn't showered or brushed my hair since early that morning. But in his appraising eyes, I could see a gleam of approval. He had to really like me to think I looked normal now. After a night and a day like the ones I'd just spent.

I smiled, then kissed him lightly on the lips. "Hope I'm not contagious."

He kissed me back sweetly, then more deeply. My heart lurched around like a drunk. The boy could really kiss.

"Missed doing that," he whispered when we finally drew apart.

I pulled him inside the apartment and closed the door. Then I followed his bulky form into the living room. He had a footballer's ass, tightly bunned, slappable. All I could think about was his broad chest pressed against my narrow one, his tender lips on mine.

"How was the maul? You get pounded?" I was faking it when I tried to talk rugby. I needed to go to some games, get fluent.

"Well, it was more like rugby light today. Meaning I'm still in one piece. Not like the ANRL."

The American National Rugby League, the big time. Firth didn't play pro ball, thank god. What a rough sport. The pro players really kicked each other's ass. They basically tried to kill one another. League tag wasn't quite so deadly. Still, injuries were the norm. You had to be a real man's man to play rugby.

My manly man said, "I'm starving, babe."

See? Told you he was a he-man. My heart kind of bump-de bumped. Like the silly little filly I am sometimes.

Then he gave me an elfish grin. "It'll be nice to have dinner with someone who isn't dribbling their food. Unless, of course, that's how you always eat?"

Firth put one muddied arm around my shoulder. He meant well. He was the kind of man who always meant well.

"You suck, dude." I tapped his chest lightly with my palm. It was damp with manly sweat, and the muscles there felt hard as stone. Yum.

He looked around. "Fer fuck's sake, who left the

window open? It's like I took a wrong turn and ended up at my place. Brrrrr. What're you doing, hiding your doobie smoke or something?" He shivered like a wimpy girl.

I laughed. "I was working. Oh my god, wait until I tell you about it."

I hurried over to the window to close it. Firth hadn't stopped at his place to shower, so all he had on were grass-stained rugby shorts and a super dirty striped jersey. He had stopped to buy me a bouquet of pale lavender lilacs, which he brought out now from behind his back.

My heart skipped around a little when he handed them to me. I was going soft, like some sorry-ass girlie chick. My legs felt loose when I walked to the kitchen, pretending to hunt for a vase.

"You're a really nice guy," was all I managed to say. I was actually choked up. Fuck me.

"That's what they all say," he responded, but he didn't laugh when he said it. "Nice guys finish last," he added. Ominously. He held himself in a tight hug, and he was shaking a little. His teeth were actually chattering. "The dirt bird gets the worm."

"Speaking of worms, let's get those noodles delivered. That way, you don't need to pick up. You can go warm up in my shower." I hustled him toward the bathroom. "You'll have to put your dirty clothes back on afterward, though. I have nothing that would fit you." I handed him a clean towel. "You like seafood with your wormy noodles?"

Firth jumped in the shower while I ordered the food. I set the table with some of Grandma Jackie's china, poured us each a frosted mug of Guinness, and lit a half-dozen candles.

When he walked into the living room, naked and freckly and really big and so bearish I could hardly sit still, I kind of gasped. "I'm having a déjà vu."

"Let's take this French thing up to the next level," he said and scooped me up. "We never did get around to it that first night. Ever since, there's been something I've been meaning to do."

His skin was like a shag rug, a reddish-gold shag rug. I rubbed myself against it, purring. Then I looked him in the eye and kissed him. I kept on kissing him until he lowered me onto my bed. He undressed me slowly, kissing me once or twice before he lay down beside me. We stared at one another. My heart bounced up and down like a kid on a trampoline.

"This is what I've been wanting to do since the minute I met you," he said.

I wrapped my arms and legs around him and kissed him some more. When he rolled on top of me, I held my breath. Would he crush me? Would he make me love him, only to abandon me? Execute the old quick split, the way everyone else I cared about did?

Firth kissed me softly, my forehead, my nose, my lips. He licked the hollow of my neck, my nipples, my armpits. He nuzzled my belly, making a slow delicious trail down to where we both really wanted him to be. When his tongue found the spot, I arched my back. "Boy oh boy."

He laughed his big man's laugh, then sucked until I came hard and long.

"Beautiful," Firth said.

He entered me slowly, carefully, the way big men do. Whoa. Incredible. When he rocked me gently, gradually increasing the speed of his thrusts, I could feel something building inside me. Something big, something powerful.

Rocking together, panting, sweating, we looked in one another's eyes. His cute freckly face was serious, caring. I felt connected. I felt *seen.*

When I started to come, he slowed just a little. "I mean this, Jacy. I'm not kidding around here."

"I know," I said, gasping. I was on the edge of something bigger than I'd ever experienced. "I trust you," I said. And I meant it.

He lifted up my ass with his huge paws, then pushed deeper inside me than I thought possible. I came with a giant shudder that, as it rippled through my body, triggered a response in him as well. Firth yelled my name, releasing with a loud roar.

We lay in a heap together on top of the sheets, catching our breath.

"That was even better than I imagined it. And I imagined it a lot," he said.

I laughed.

Firth rolled over to look in my eyes again. I stroked his flushed cheeks.

"I'm so grateful to be here with you," he said.

I kissed him slowly, like I meant it. Because I did.

****

Later, over moo shi shrimp, fried rice, and lobster lo mein, I told Firth about the manuscript. The plot, the characters, the lucid, real-life writing style. He let me rattle on and on while he chowed down. His after-game appetite was huge. Or maybe it was his after-sex appetite.

Finally, he shoved his chair back, patted his bare

stomach contentedly, and belched.

"Good one," I said. "I like a man who can let 'er rip."

He smiled. "You got yourself one of those."

We were both naked, still warm from our lovemaking, heated up again from the spicy food.

Firth burped several more times, and I giggled. He was so much himself that I knew him already. Firth was Firth. Such a wonderful change from the men I had known and not loved. Such a wonderful change from my own family. From me. I felt like I might actually know Firth better than I knew myself.

"So, is this the project you were working on with the old guy?" he asked.

I served myself the rest of the greasy lo mein noodles. "Yeah. Why?"

Firth sipped his beer. "Bear with me now. I don't understand publishing, I'm just a lowly city worker, down in the stinky trenches with the rest of the trash. But I'm thinking, if you got paid to write a book for this guy, then isn't it his property? Like, who owns the copyright? Whose name goes on the cover? Whose story is it?"

Good question. "It's his property ultimately, I guess. But he didn't pay me. I did this one on spec."

Firth snorted. "Fer fuck's sake. You know better than that, don't you? Never work on anything on spec. I don't know the writing biz, but in every other business, it's always a terrible idea to do anything without upfront money. Not unless you're willing to get majorly poled."

He shook his head, frowned, and looked worried. Like he actually cared whether I got poled by some client. Who had no money because he was dead already, a ghost. Could I get screwed by a dead guy? Could that even happen?

"But hey, you have a contract, right? Something on paper?"

I shrugged. I didn't want him to think I was an idiot, but what good would a contract do if my client existed in some other dimension?

Firth raised his brows, shook his head again, and sighed. He thought I was being stupid. I hate it when a man thinks I'm just another dumb broad. That really pisses me off. So I decided to tell him the truth. About me and JD.

Swallowing a chewy lobster chunk, I thought carefully about how I could word this bizarre self-disclosure. How would a normal guy react to such a strange story from his new lover? Would he freak out? Laugh at me? Suggest medication? Was I willing to risk it? Firth judging me, finding me lacking? And the approval I'd seen in his keen blue eyes? What if that changed? Faded away, morphing into disapproval, disgust?

I cleared my throat. I felt like Austin, about to address a jury. "There's something I need to tell you."

"Uh oh. I hate it when a girl says that. Especially right after we've made wild, passionate love. Especially when she has moo shi on her really adorable chin."

I wiped at the grease with my napkin. "It's not what you think. In fact, it's not the kind of thing you've heard before. From a girl or anyone else." I pushed my plate away and took a swig of warm beer. "My old client, the guy who dictated the book I'm editing now? I think I told you he's an author, right? Well, he's actually a very famous writer. And, well…he's also a dead one. He's a ghost. A ghost writer."

Firth looked at me, a half-smile lingering on his lips. Did I tell you he has really nice lips? Pillowy. And right now they were wet. Yum.

When I didn't say anything else, Firth's smile faded away. "You're serious," he said, his voice full of surprise.

I nodded. "Dead serious."

We both snickered.

He rubbed a big hand across his mussy hair. Sometimes, in just the right light, Firth looked like he had a little flame ablaze on his scalp. I love red hair. Bright, fiery hair.

Firth cocked his head and grinned at me. "You are one interesting chick. Weird, but very, very interesting."

I took that as a compliment. I needed all the compliments I could get. "So, since dead men tell no tales and all that, I think I own the legal rights to the tale the dead man told me. Right?"

Firth stopped smiling. "Maybe. Unless he has heirs to his estate. And they claim the right to works based on his writing, his characters, as part of their estate. Which in some cases, with certain authors, is probably worth a ton of money." He shrugged. "I ain't no lawyer. But you might want to consult one about this stuff. An intellectual property rights type. Armani suit, four hundred dollars an hour."

I nodded. He was probably right. But, except for Austin, I didn't know anyone in the legal profession. I didn't have the money to spend on a Manhattan law firm, and I had no desire to contact my ex. "I guess I'll try to find a literary agent to represent the book. They'll know about intellectual property rights law. I'll let them tell me what I can and can't do."

He nodded. "That'll work." Then he leaned forward and grabbed my hand, which disappeared in his great big bear paw. "Jacy, it's so great to see you so passionate about your project. Reminds me of the night we met."

How so? *What did I say, what did I do, how did I win your heart?*

We looked at one another. The candles were burning low, snuffing themselves out one by one. It was getting harder to see each other, lending an air of freedom and daring to our discussion. Like we were sitting around the campfire, sharing secrets.

He must have picked up on my willingness, my openness. He meant well, I'm sure. But he read me wrong. All wrong.

"You're a brave woman, Jacy," he said, squeezing my hand. "I work with abused people every day. Some of them never get beyond their pain and hurt. They damage themselves, continuing their childhood suffering all their lives. You've worked hard to recover. To find your passion, to be creative with your past. I admire you for that. I know how hard it is to get beyond psychic pain."

Psychic pain? "You mean Mother?" I asked. Psychic pain in the ass, maybe.

"I mean the death of your brother. Your father's depression, his suicide. Your own mental instability. All you went through, all the heavy emotional shit, all without the kind of support you needed. You're tough, Jacy. Tough and brave."

I flinched, withdrawing my hand to cover my mouth. It felt like he'd slapped me across the face. We stared at one another for a long moment.

"I think you have me mixed up with somebody else. Some other girl." I turned away from his laser stare. I got up to fetch myself another beer. I didn't need to offer him one. I already knew what he'd say.

I rummaged around in the refrigerator and grabbed two bottles. "Where did you get your information about me, anyway? I sound like one of your case reports."

Firth sighed. "Don't be like this. When you told me about your family, what you'd been through, all I could think was, this chick is the most truthful person I've ever met." He paused while I cracked open the beers. "You haven't seemed willing to talk about this stuff again, though. Not since that first night. Maybe you decided you didn't trust me. I'm hoping now you do. Trust me."

I handed him a beer. "I trust you, Firth. I already told you that. But this shit about my brother? My dad committing suicide? I don't have any idea what you're talking about. I just visited them. At West 87th. Except for having to deal with my bitchy mother, they're both fine."

Firth shot up and out of his seat. Boom! He'd tipped the table precariously, extinguishing what was left of the candles and knocking food containers on their sides. Greasy sauce spread across the tabletop and dripped onto the floor. I'd heard stories about redheads with tempers and, believe me, all the rumors are true. These people are like firebombs when they get mad. Everything goes up in a convulsion of inflammatory rage. Whoa.

Vixie sprang from the couch and dashed off to hide. I felt like following him, rolling under my bed, and burying myself in the dust piles. Firth was glaring at me. I'm sure I shrank back in fear. I'd never seen him angry before. Wow.

"Fuck me, man! Either you're lying to me now. Or you were lying to me then. What's it gonna be, girl? Headfucks or real fucking life?"

Before I could think that one through, he stomped off to the bathroom to retrieve his muddy rugby clothes. He cursed the whole time he was dressing, and at one point, it sounded like he kicked something. My wicker hamper, maybe. Later, when I went into the room to check, nothing was damaged. All hot bluster, that guy.

I wanted to say something to prevent him from leaving. Firth was the first man I'd really felt anything for. I wanted to trust him, to feel safe in his arms. To feel safe in his life. Our life. But what could I say? He had my story wrong. What he'd said about my family and me? It was fiction. A fever dream. That wasn't my life.

"Call me if you want to have a real relationship," he said on his way out the door. "Otherwise, go fuck yourself."

First, I drank my beer, then I drank his. After that, I polished off the rest of the beers in the refrigerator. Yeah, I finished up all his Guinnies. Firth wouldn't be back to drink them.

I sat on my couch in a buzzy trance, not thinking, just drinking. Yellow light from the street outside rivered across the floor. In the distance, car horns blared and ambulances raced by. People in the alley below shouted and laughed. Someone rustled through the dumpster.

After all the beer was gone, I went to bed. I left the spilled Chinese food all over the table, right where Firth's temper had knocked it.

****

In the morning, my head felt fat and bruised. My brain pulsed like a bad tooth. Maybe I needed to have it yanked out of my stupid skull.

When I dragged myself out to the living room, I nearly wept. My bouquet of delicate lilacs had wilted in the water glass I'd used as a vase. Tiny browned petals littered the coffee table. I hadn't added enough water. I'd been so excited, so flattered, so nervous. So crazy about Firth.

Vixie must have gotten into the greasy noodles. There were darling little puddles of cat puke and cat shit all over the living room floor.

You should have seen it. It was so bad I almost laughed.

Chapter Ten

I wasn't going to tell you about all this. About Renew. Because I really don't want to go into it, to tell you the truth. But in the name of full disclosure, self-revelation for the purpose of wholeness or closure or whatever, I guess I have to include this stuff. It's the part of my life I'm most embarrassed about.

You have no idea how humiliating it was. Being there. At that awful place.

Renew. What a fucking name. Corny, right? But I had to admit, it had a bit of a draw. Who doesn't want to renew themselves? And at the time, I was aware that I needed something. I needed to make some major changes in my life.

I thought I'd been covering up the shit pretty well, but I hadn't been. Once Firth dumped me, I totally lost it. Stopped going in to work. Stopped pretending I was writing the next great American novel. Stopped most everything.

You know how that happens, right? You go along every day, doing what you need to do, getting by, talking to your friends about nothing, learning nothing, experiencing the nothingness of it all. Always smiling, pretending it's okay. Yes indeed, these are the things you do. Until you simply can't anymore. You can't fucking fake it anymore.

Once I stopped getting out of bed, I could no

longer pretend I had it going on. I couldn't fool myself anymore. I knew that, as JD might say, my faculties were no longer intact.

One cold winter day, Mother called. She told me to pack a week's worth of summer clothes and wait for the airport limousine. "I'm sending you to a Florida health spa, dear. The limo will be there in an hour. So, unless you want to come home again, live here with me, you will be ready when it arrives."

It was all I could do to not turn over on my side and go back to sleep. But the idea of a little spa vacation, a week of warmth and relaxation, gradually leaked into my psyche and roused me from my stupor. I had a choice to make. What would it be—87th Street hell or some fancy pampering down in sunny Florida?

I chose the sunshine state.

Somehow I made it out the front door after the limo arrived. But at LaGuardia, I was so out of it I almost missed my plane. I sat there in a plastic chair in the bustling airport, a worn copy of *L'Etranger* in my lap. I read little and understood none of the words, the beautiful French words. Inside my head, I was drifting.

I don't remember much about the flight. The middle-aged woman next to me patted my hand when we landed. I remember that. Such a tender gesture, I felt like crying. Maybe I did cry. I don't really remember.

The terminal in Fort Lauderdale was packed with people in loud clothes. Light clothes. Skimpy clothes. Short shorts and tight tanks tops. Bathing suits and tiny skirts. Flip-flops. People wore sandals, open-toed casual shoes. No black, no boots. There was something buoyant in the air. There were so many tanned, laughing faces. It felt like summer vacation.

A stocky man in a flowered Hawaiian shirt stood waiting for me in the baggage claim area. He held up a hand-printed sign that said "Renew." People glanced at it as they passed by him. Maybe they thought he was a Jesus freak or something.

"I'm Tad," he said to me as we waited by the carousel for my luggage to arrive. He wore mirrored shades. He was bulky, and he smelled like aftershave. "I'm just the driver, so don't ask me any questions about the program."

Okay.

When I pointed to my duffle bag, he grabbed it. Then I followed him out of the baggage area. He walked fast.

When we exited the air-conditioned terminal, the heat was intense. The sun slapped me awake. Wow, that Florida sunshine really hit hard. It was relentless, searing your skin. And I was shocked by the thickness of the air. It felt like entering a rain forest, a jungle of heat. I was sweating in my black long-sleeved tee and jeans.

We made our way through the parking garage. It was full of tall, colorful plants. You could hear these small decorative waterfalls splashing and, now and again, a smattering of bird song. Flowers bloomed everywhere, white petals clutching deep green vines. It smelled sweet and heady. Like jasmine.

A part of me relaxed. This place was different, so different from the dark nothingness of New York. It felt like something at least, like something vibrant. Something real.

"Here we go," Tad said over one thick shoulder. He popped the trunk of a car the size of a small boat and tossed in my bag. "Lap belts only," he told me when I climbed into the passenger seat. "This baby's an antique."

His shiny white Cadillac El Dorado sped north on the interstate, weaving in and out of traffic. For an old guy, Tad drove pretty fast. Every once in a while, one of those kamikaze motorcycles would scream past us, doing at least ninety. It was stupid, but I liked it. I sank back against the leather headrest, smiling.

"You want to stop for dinner before we get there?" Tad streaked into the right lane, cutting off a battered van. "You won't like the food at Renew. You might want to take advantage now while you still can."

He already had his blinker on, so I said okay, as if it mattered to me. But really, I didn't care. I was just happy to have the car window open, the hot wind in my face.

We pulled off the interstate and drove east on a wide throughway. Palm trees decorated the crowded asphalt streets. Traffic was heavy, mean spirited. Pedestrians wore dark glasses, brightly colored shorts, and bathing suits. The sun glazed the sidewalks, bouncing off the pavement and into my eyes. I didn't have sunglasses with me, and I needed them.

Tad parked in front of a strip mall, next to a lot of other shiny coupes and convertibles. "You like Applebee's?" he asked, then shoved open his door.

No answer was expected. He eased out of his side of the car, so I climbed out of mine.

Crossing the black tar lot, I started to sweat. The sun hit me like a lightning bolt. It was brutal. I'd inherited my family's super white skin, none of us able to tan. I wondered if I'd be spending a lot of time tending to painful sunburns while at Renew. I didn't dare ask Tad, though. It didn't seem like the kind of thing he'd be willing to discuss.

I followed him inside the restaurant, where it was cool and dark. We waited quietly for the hostess to seat us.

I had no idea what time it was or even the day of the week. Right before I got on the plane, I'd reached my personal vanishing point. Waiting in the terminal, not reading Camus, I felt totally invisible. Did I even exist? If I did, then why?

Now, here in another world, a brighter, more vivid world, I started to feel more solid. In the crowded restaurant, I could feel others' eyes skate over me. The old men in their lollipop-hued shirts and Bermuda shorts, these guys looked me up and down. I existed; there was proof.

When we were seated in a butterscotch vinyl booth, Tad stared at me. His eyes were dark blue, like the winter ocean I'd been flying above. We regarded one another across the narrow table.

"You don't look like the other girls. The Renew chicks," he said.

His white-gray brush cut and prominent handle-bar mustache gave Tad the aura of a shoot-from-the-hip ex-cop. I figured he'd tell me what was on his mind only when he wanted to, but I could probably trust it.

"How so?" I asked, pretending to be interested in the menu. Weren't these wellness spas all the same?

"You know how they work the meal thing there?" he asked.

"No. I don't know anything about the program. Nothing." I shrugged.

Everything had been arranged by my mother. I'd agreed to go only because I was too exhausted to say no.

"When the waitress comes, order a full meal," Tad advised. "Soup, salad, dinner, dessert. Drinks, if you want. If you're old enough. You *are* over twenty-one, right?"

I nodded.

"You don't look it," he said.

Whatever. I really could use a drink. I ordered the grilled chicken special and a Cosmopolitan. Tad asked the perky waitress for a Heineken and a basket of onion rings. Called her *darlin'*. He was that kind of man.

Still, I decided I liked him. So I asked a string of questions, and once in a while, he answered me.

"Renew caters to young women, teens and twenty-somethings, some older gals. They're like skeletons, most of them girls. Or they're big old cows with tree trunk waists and round red faces. They all walk around in hospital outfits, but none of 'em are sick. Strangest damn place I ever seen." He shook his head. "I feel sorry as hell for their families. Most of these women are freaks. It's the god-awful truth."

Okay, so this trip was less vacay and more rehab. That figured. Mother was never one for fun.

Tad looked me in the eye. I was sipping my drink, loving the buzz I was getting but trying not to be the fool about it.

He twirled his mustache with his thick fingers. "You, though. You don't fit. What's wrong with you, anyway?"

I shrugged. "Stress. Family and boyfriend problems. A while back I dropped out of grad school, got a shit job. I've been lying around too much, feeling depressed. That kind of stuff." I poked the limp salad with my fork. It reminded me of the fake-looking bagged lettuce Mother always bought. "I thought Renew was a spa. You think I'll be weirded out by the place?"

"Darlin', I can't tell you much. I drive the girls back and forth from the airport or pick 'em up at their homes if they live in the area. A lot of them come from very wealthy families. You ought to see the palaces these people live in. You'd think with all that money they might be able to—" He wiped the beer froth off his lips. "Sorry. Didn't mean to offend."

I shrugged. Again. I seemed to do nothing but shrug with old Tad. "I know, don't worry about it. But what's with the food at Renew? I mean, am I going to be able to order a pizza if I need one?"

He frowned. "Don't know, little lady. All I know is what I hear while I'm behind the wheel. All them girls complain about the food. Ask me to drive 'em to Dunkin' Donuts, Mickey D's, the mall for frozen yogurt. That kind of thing." He sized me up, sat back against the seat, hiccupped a few times. "You look like the kind of gal who appreciates a heads up. S'why I'm givin' you one."

Whatever that meant. But I did appreciate the meal and I told him so.

There wasn't much else Tad could tell me, so I ate up and finished my drink. Even snarfed a few of his greasy, crunchy onion rings.

I didn't know what to expect at Renew, but how bad could it be? If it was intolerable, I'd just check myself out and fly back to New York. In the meantime,

I wasn't semi-comatose anymore. In fact, I felt pretty good.

Hanging with Tad at Applebee's turned out to be the highlight of my visit to sunny Florida, however. The rest of my time there sucked. In fact, it's kind of a depressing story. You'll get depressed just reading about it. Booby hatches are not the most upbeat places. If you can avoid it, don't get locked up in one. And don't ever go to a glitzy laughing academy with a corny name like Renew. Or New Life. Or Verve. That kind of phony name. Believe me, you'll be sorry if you do. I can guarantee it.

Tad paid the check and waved away my cash when I held it out. "Catch me next time."

We drove west on the wide boulevard into a brazen sunset more vivid orange than anything you could see in Manhattan. I swear I could smell the salt water, even though Tad said the ocean was like ten miles away. Still, the hot breeze sure smelled like briny clams.

"There it is," Tad said.

We had just exited off the main drag into a cookie-cutter development of ranch-style suburban homes. He pointed to a Pepto-Bismol sprawl of a building in the distance, a you-can't-miss-it institutional construction squatting on a small hill. Renew was definitely not a health spa. It was an eyesore. A kind of primped up funny farm.

We turned up the long drive. I should've been angry or freaked out or scared. But I wasn't. *Whatever.* That was what I felt at the moment. Because anything was better than lying in my apartment feeling nothing.

"Except for the folks who work here and the ones who get locked up, nobody knows what the hell goes on in there. The pink castle on the hill," he said with a dramatic shake of his head. "Top secret treatments." He winked at me.

"I'll tell you everything that happens to me in there, Tad. Then you'll know all the top secrets of Renew."

We both snorted.

He parked the Caddy under a neon pink awning and carried my bag inside the revolving glass doors. Then he gave me a quick nod and left me there.

I never saw Tad again.

****

The lady at the front desk reminded me of my Aunt Jane. Austere is one way to describe her. Coolly detached would be another. Her make-up mask was heavy, her nails long and dark red, her scent pervasive and expensive. She confiscated my cell phone and handed me a clipboard with routine paperwork.

When I returned the clipboard to her, she told me to follow her. She would take me to my room.

I said nothing and did as I was told.

The plastic name tag on the jacket of her fawn-colored rayon suit said Mrs. Passern. Even though she looked like my aunt, the woman scared me. I could tell she was sick of younger women and their hysterics. She didn't suffer fools. And it sure seemed like I might be one of them. Otherwise, I wouldn't be tagging along behind her down a long narrow hall. Walking past steel door after door, institutional room after room, cell after cell. I wouldn't be in need of what was sure to come. Because Mrs. Passern was going to shut me in one of these rooms, lock me in a bare cell under a naked bulb next to a folding cot and an open toilet. That was my fate, and it was sealed. Why? Because I was an insufferable fool.

The hallway smelled like pan-fried cod and fresh piss. And it was deserted. Maybe everyone was locked in their crumby cells in an over-medicated daze. I was too afraid to ask. Mrs. Passern's heels clicked on the dingy white tile. My sneakers were soundless. I waved a hand in front of my face, just to make sure I hadn't disappeared. I was there, all right. But I didn't want to be.

When we reached the last room at the far end of the hall, Mrs. Passern stopped and knocked. The door had a hollow ring to it. She opened it without using a key. I followed her in, holding my breath, ready for the worst.

The room was small, maybe twelve by twenty, a tight squeeze for more than one occupant. But it was neat, clean, the paint a light rose with white trim. No pictures or mirrors, nothing on the walls. Twin beds, two cheap looking bureaus, a single desk and straight-back chair, a double closet without doors. Clothes had been stuffed into one side of the closet, kids' shoes lined up in front on the thin mauve carpeting. One big window with slatted blinds—no bars—overlooked the parking lot. The last dregs of the setting sun streamed in.

No locks, no bars. I sighed with relief.

"I'll leave you to settle in, Jacqueline." She consulted her watch, a delicate gold band with a small crystal face. A rich person's timepiece. "Dinner is over in fifteen minutes. If you wish to eat something, you should go to the cafeteria immediately."

"Jacy," I said. "I'm not hungry. Thanks."

She appraised me with her cool eyes. Her eyelids

were dusted the same shade, a strange teal hue. "That's your option, Jacqueline. But after tonight, you will need to eat all of your meals with the other patients. In the cafeteria."

"Jacy," I said.

But she'd already turned her back to me. I could hear her heels tapping on the tile as she marched back to her post.

I unpacked what I had stuffed in the duffel on my way out the door. A light summer dress, a pair of white jeans, denim cut-offs, T-shirts, panties, socks. Slippers and a cotton nightgown. My hairbrush, toiletries. Sunblock. A black bikini. Aqua flip-flops.

I stood by my half of the closet and looked around the room. Could've been worse, but still. On anyone's to-do list, a batshit bin is not the place to go.

Fortunately, exits seemed to be everywhere. I walked to the window. First floor room, pop-out screen that could be easily removed, lots of thick bushes to hide one's escape. Seemed simple enough. There was nothing to stop me from—

"Holy shitsky. You're here!" a screechy voice behind me yelled. I turned around. A tiny girl ran across the room and sprang into my arms. "Yippee," she screeched. "I'm Kristi. I've been waiting for you *all day*."

She was light as a baby bird, all air-filled bones and soft fluff. I held her by the waist, a pencil-thin joke of a waist, and she wrapped her knobby thighs around my hips, clinging to me. Her pixie face was covered with a pale, downy fuzz. I've not seen eyes that big and round since.

"You won't be here long. You're too normal,"

Kristi predicted instantly. She lowered her voice. "I overheard them talking about you. Reactive depression. That's a short-term diagnosis." She threw back her head and laughed. Some of her molars were missing. "I'm long-term. Dual diagnosis. How was the trip down? You tired? You like chocolate?"

She talked fast, moving from subject to subject without a pause. I was having a hard time keeping up. I shrugged, jiggling her so she slid down my hips to my thighs.

Kristi laughed again. "You don't have an eating disorder! If you did, you'd absolutely be addicted to chocolate."

She let her sticklike legs drop down and set her small feet on the floor. Then we stood looking at one another. She was maybe five feet tall and probably half my weight. Her hands and feet, her body, were like those of an undernourished child. I thought of what Tad had told me about some of the girls at Renew—skeletal.

Right. Bone dolls. I was like a fat pony in comparison. She came up to my chin. The kids' shoes in the front of the closet? Hers.

"I brought you some food from dinner. In case you're hungry." My new roommate removed a napkin-wrapped packet from the front pocket of her baggy cargo shorts. She perched on one of the identical beds and unfolded the squashed package to reveal a flattened sandwich on white bread. "Peanut butter and butter. Spread extra thick. I made it for you. You like?"

Uh, no. Me no like.

"Not hungry. I already ate," I told her.

She giggled. "That's what we all say."

She jumped up and hurried past me. With a quick

tug, she opened the window and, using both hands, began rubbing the sandwich against the screen. Pushing the bread through the small wire holes, forcing the food to sieve though to the outside.

"I don't want to eat it," she explained over her shoulder.

Of course not. That would make her fat.

I tried not to roll my eyes. I'd gone to school with girls like this, girls afraid of food, obsessed with eating and not eating. That anorexic thing the rich women did on the Upper West Side. My own mother's self-starvation behaviors. Ugh.

I sighed. It was going to be a long week. It was going to feel like forever.

Chapter Eleven

I wasn't stuck at Renew forever, but sometimes it felt like it. I don't want to tell you all of it because, I swear to god, it will bore you to tears. Who wants a detailed rundown on my time in the nuthatch? Do you really want to hear about a bunch of wealthy fucked-up women mired in hysterical gloom?

You know how some people can't help themselves? Well, some people help themselves to everything. Put those two kinds of women together in a locked ward, and you've got Renew.

Time dragged. Then it sped up during the few key events that led to my swift departure.

To my surprise, my kooky little roommate turned out to be one of the more enjoyable inpatients at that god-awful place. I could talk to her, she had a twisted sense of humor similar to mine, and she was respectful of my personal space. Yes, she liked to leap into my arms whenever she saw me. But she did that to everyone she took a liking to. And Kristi really liked me. We had one another's back. That anchored me.

However, after the first week, enough was enough. I really didn't know why I had to stay any longer than that. I'd already endured a long, difficult, and eye-opening seven days of institutional life. Talk about fascist attitudes. The Renew staff outdid old Mussolini. Their rigid activities schedule was sacred, staff and patients were given their orders, all rules were to be obeyed. No discussion. Line up one by one for showers, meals, therapy. Repeat.

Renew demanded absolute sheeple behavior. Bleat, bleat.

Mother had refused to take my calls all week. I hung out at the bay of battered, graffitied pay phones in a dingy cubicle off the cafeteria. I spent an hour there every night after dinner, dialing and redialing angrily. Letting my mother's phone ring and ring and ring. Such a hollow sound. She successfully avoided me.

Every time I slammed the plastic receiver into the cradle, I earned scolding stares from the dinner duty staff. Fuck them, I was allowed to make my calls.

After seven straight nights of this game, Mother finally picked up. I almost hung up on her, I was so pissed off.

"They advised me not to talk to you during your first week," she said defensively. "So you could adjust. Have you adjusted?"

I wanted to rip her head off. "You admitted me to an eating disorders facility, Mother. I'm depressed, not anorexic. Whatever were you thinking?" I was fuming. Something smoky shot out my ears.

"It doesn't matter, dear. Renew has an excellent psychiatric staff and a marvelous reputation. You sound better already."

That might have been true. I'd done nothing but eat, sleep, and talk about myself to shrinks, social workers, psychology students, and other patients with nothing else to do but listen to my self-absorbed prattle. And share their own self-absorbed thoughts. After a few days of that kind of expressive freedom, I'd discovered how angry I was with my mother. I'd uncovered the root of my neurosis, as one psychiatric social worker put it.

Mother bashing was a blood sport at Renew.

"This is the kind of thing you do to me that has contributed to my depression, Mother. Your deceit. Your self-protective lying. It's all about you. Never about my needs. Never has been," I sputtered.

She tsked.

"They're encouraging me to explore what I want, rather than continue to do only what is expected of me," I explained. Your brain has to be cold. Full of cold, cold thoughts. I clung to this concept and it calmed me. "How many versions of yourself have you discarded over the years, Mother? Think about it. I'm in the process of abandoning a self that is *not* real. That does *not* work for me."

She started screaming. I had to hold the phone away from my ear.

"I'm spending thousands of dollars for this? What nonsense! Where are you getting this gobbledygook? Are you making things up again, Jacqueline?"

"I'm locked up in a madhouse, Mother. And I'm suicidally depressed. You call that gobbledygook?"

I was exaggerating. I was only clinically depressed, like millions of my fellow Americans. We don't like our lives, but we don't necessarily want to give them up.

Mother hung up on me. But to my surprise, she did not call the administrator to have me shipped home. Maybe she thought my accusations were nothing more than additional symptoms of my craziness. Maybe she thought I'd eventually be cured of my outlandish ideas.

Maybe she figured that, soon enough, the counselors would convince me of a mother's essential goodness. After all, she was paying for my mental health, so she probably thought my recovery would include a free pass for her.

Who knows what she thought? I remained at Renew until I fled. On foot. Which was after almost a month of trapped boredom, the most rest I'd had in years, and an intense immersion in both my own damaged psyche and my fellow inmates' full-blown lunacy. All that time, I kept my cool. Somehow. But I was privy to some of the most eye-opening extremes of self-destructive behavior. By other residents, not by me. Screaming tantrums, shit fits, painful hair pulling, cutting at limbs with plastic utensils. Cat fights. Head banging. All night wailing at the moon. Bughouse stuff. When I tell you I was the sane one of the bunch, I am not bragging. Or kidding. I'm not even lying for a change.

I might still be imprisoned in the Pepto-Bismol castle, awaiting my release, if Kristi hadn't gone off the edge. My time at Renew was torturous, boring and painful and awful, but it was helping me to look at who I'd become. I'd begun thinking about how I could make an alternative selection. I was learning how I could choose another version of myself and go with that for a while.

But it was my tiny roommate who ended up vaulting me into the next phase of my life, changing me forever.

The night had started out like all the others on the ward. Enforced dullness, punctuated by brief periods of intense chaos. Medicated quiet, interrupted by the occasional ear-piercing scream of anguish. Once in a while, a scrawny figure in a johnny racing down the sterile hall.

My body had adapted to the cocktail of meds we were served daily. So I was lethargic, like most of us were, thanks to the required doses of pharmaceutical calm, our chemical straitjackets. But I could tell I was getting mentally stronger. I could feel my anger, the fiery ire that had lurked deep inside me for so long. All that bitter bile, it had begun to spit out in talk therapy. Now it was hardening up, forming a kind of protective shell.

Now I knew who I hated and why. Now I understood who had died, and who I blamed for that.

My roommate and I had endured another bland but filling dinner, and we were hanging out in our room. Kristi was in a low mood. She'd been subdued for days, ever since she heard about her sister's engagement party. Kristi's sister was a college student up in Gainesville, a cheerleader, pre-med, a real go-getter. The kind of girl who could eat like a normal person, make good grades, make love, make plans. Which made things worse for Kristi.

We were both drifting along, spacing out or talking quietly, the way we liked to, when Mary-Alicia appeared in the doorway. On our floor, bedroom doors were never locked. We left ours open when we were there, unless it was after lights out. Might as well give up your privacy voluntarily. It was better than having staff walk in on you dozens of times a day. Patients had to be accepting of constant supervision, ready for inspection at any time. Taking a shower without a curtain was humbling. Taking a dump while under guard was totally humiliating. We were constantly suspected of breaking the rules, hiding food or flushing it away, purging ourselves in a variety of icky ways. I don't want to go into it. You'll be disgusted if I do.

Renew inpatients were not supposed to be able to get away with anything. Yet, that's pretty much how the majority of residents spent their time. Always trying to get away with as much insane behavior as they could. It was like a game. A challenge for a bunch of bored women, one most of them took on with creative ingenuity and great gusto.

Hide the mashed potato in your sock, hide the gravy in your robe, who wants to play hide the roast beef in the toilet?

"Guys, you won't believe the new girl," Mary-Alicia announced. Her chins bounced when she talked, one of her most distracting features. "She's a model! Totally gorgeous. She has a tattoo. Her boyfriend's name. It's on her butthole."

Kristi and I sat up at the same time. "No way," we said. No way! How could you even—

"Yes way."

Mary-Alicia pushed herself through the doorway, squeezing her Tweedle-Dee torso into our desk chair. The pale green johnny rode up her thighs, and her hammy flesh seeped over the sides of the narrow wooden chair.

"She'll show it to you if you want to see it. Daniel Fresk. That's his name. I guess she lets him stick it in there."

Her apple cheeks flushed with embarrassed glee. Mary-Alicia's father was a copper mining millionaire. He owned mines all over the world. She was thirty, single, richer than Trump, and totally unzipped mentally. The woman had bizarre bordering on scary food obsessions and a stalking disorder, or something like that. She'd stalked Susie Ormond. Then J.K. Rowling. She was so rich she had a global reach for her screwball whims.

We tolerated her, though. Why not? And occasionally she had excellent entertainment value.

"I heard she's in for self-mutilation. Cutting. She's very beautiful," Mary-Alicia said wistfully.

That was another thing about Renew. The more fucked up you were, the higher your popularity score. It sounded like the new girl would be moving into a top slot.

"I'm sure she's quite the babe," Kristi said, rolling her eyes at me. "Another bored narcissist living an unsubstantial life, tattooing her exhaust equipment, wallowing in her arrested development."

"Anal stage fixation," I added. Kristi nodded, encouraging. "Childhood abuse. Attention Surplus Disorder."

We laughed. Kristi and I were sick to death of diagnoses, personality disorders, overblown analyses of the historical, gender-based, and socioeconomic reasons for what we saw as our right to self-express. In any way we saw fit. Someone wanted to carve her navel with bloody Xs, solder rings to her labia, needlepoint a guy's name on her private parts? Go for it, was our reaction. Go. For. It.

If you were subjected to being watched and analyzed, labeled and scolded, critiqued and judged every second of every day for weeks, months, years, you might adopt a similar radical attitude. Maybe not.

But people are always ruining things for others, for everyone who seems just too different. What business is it of ours? Why do we care? Why not leave them the hell alone? If we all did exactly that, places like Renew wouldn't exist.

Believe me, that would be a good thing.

"I want to meet the new girl," Kristi announced. "Go get her, M.A. Bring her down. We'll have some hooch. Toast her arrival here on fuckup hall."

Mary-Alicia struggled to her feet, sighing. "Well, okay, I'll try to talk her into it. But she's in kind of a bad mood."

"We'll cheer her up," Kristi said, holding a skinny thumb and finger to her lips, pretending to do a shot. She had a plastic jug full of vodka hidden in the back of our closet in a boot box. Once in a while, we shut our door and snuck a little snort, which was fun. "Bring her down and we can all compare assholes. Like we do in group therapy. Stare up each other's butts and make stupid comments."

"Okay, yeah. I'll see what I can do," Mary-Alicia said, waddling to the door. "No promises."

"Whatever," I said, dismissing her.

I was already bored. Mary-Alicia could be boring. The new girl and her inked ass would probably bore me, too. Kristi didn't bore me, though. She was bright, strange, and funny. Unpredictable.

"If she doesn't show up in five, let's us do a shot," I suggested.

"You are on it, girl." Kristi propped herself up against the headboard. Her neck was like a pipe cleaner, long and thin and fuzzy. Her head dawdled, like she barely had the strength to hold it steady.

I lay back down on my bed. "What do you think about this? Okay, so they tell us we're supposed to listen to our inner voice, right? Like there's somebody there inside you who's wise and everything, ready to tell you what to do. Well, if you're supposed to go within and then you do and... What if nobody's in there? What if *you* are all you got?"

We talked about shit like this. The unreliable self. Psychological headfucks. How we wanted nothing, but we wanted a lot of it.

"I know," she said. "I've been thinking like that lately, too. I've been thinking, like if there is someone there, what if whoever is in there, the spirit or soul or whoever, what if it's evil? Out to get you. Ruin you. So that inner voice they're always telling us to listen to? Maybe we shouldn't listen to it."

She moved to the end of my bed and grabbed my feet. I had my flip-flops on. I refused to wear a johnny and hospital slippers. Instead, every day I dressed for the beach I never got to see. The ocean was less than a dozen miles east. Some nights I could smell it, the salty tang of frothy waves on clean white sand. The world was out there, fresh and beautiful. Yet here we sat. Prisoners in this suburban castle, in the unreal world, in our own fucked-up lives.

"If we can't listen to ourselves, Jacy, who do we listen to? What are we supposed to do?"

"I know," I concurred. "Like, I'm wondering if there's something else inside each of us that can guide us better than whatever or whoever we've got. Something wiser than the inner voice that has been doing such a fucked-up job. I mean, if we choose another self to be, an alternate self, do we end up with a different inner voice? Or what?"

"Yeah." Kristi nodded eagerly. She pinched my big toe with her little chicken-bone fingers. "I thought the same thing. But I listen and listen and listen. And it's the same old voice. You look ugly. You eat like a hog. Your belly is huge. I'm not even twenty-one years old yet, and I've been listening to this shit for a decade. I have no breasts, no periods. I've never had a boyfriend, never even been kissed. I dropped out of school in tenth grade. I'm forever unemployable. I am sick to death of myself, of whoever is talking to me like that, keeping me trapped in my own head."

The light from the parking lot gave her anemic skin a buttery hue. Her beautiful eyes took up most of her small face, but there was a flatness in them. She'd lost more mass since I'd moved in. Maybe it was a nutritional issue, but it seemed as if she were leaving. Like the life was leaking out of her.

She clasped my ankle in a tweezery grip. "If I don't weigh eighty tomorrow, they're gonna move me upstairs to R-ward."

I'd known this was coming. Kristi never ate more than a couple small mouthfuls of food at any meal. The threats to force-feed were constant; the staff had reached their limits and wanted to put a halt to her self-starvation. R-ward meant bed restriction with enforced feeding. Tube feedings through the nose. So she wouldn't die.

The other girls thought this was horrible. I thought it made perfect sense. I wanted Kristi to get better. I wanted her to live.

"I'd rather die than go lie in a hospital bed all day," she said.

There was fear in her voice. And shame.

I leaned forward to pat her feathery head. I liked to pet her like a small bird. Tenderly.

Usually, I refrained from telling her what to do. It was too easy for me. I'd gained at least ten pounds since my arrival. I looked forward to meals and ate whatever they served me. The food was blah, nutritionally balanced, copious, and unimaginative. Compared to the psychic drain of therapy and the dullness of lying around in our room, however, meal times were the highlight of our days.

But that was my personal view. For girls who couldn't eat or struggled with binging whenever they did eat, mealtimes at Renew were hell. Hell in the form of power smoothies thickened with creamy protein powders, high-fat spreads on carbohydrate chunks, hidden ingredients and proscribed servings that were, depending on your issues, either way too big or way too small. When you were a control freak, the mealtimes at Renew were pure unadulterated torture.

Which is why Tad thought I'd need a last meal before I checked in. The Applebee's stopover had been kind of him. But wrong. The food at Renew wasn't an issue for me. So even though I tried to understand where Kristi and the other inmates were coming from, it was difficult. The choice seemed so stark. Choose life. Don't leave the people who love you.

Still, if Kristi was faced with the choice of eating breakfast or abandoning me for the restricted ward, I was hoping my roommate could just choke down some cafeteria food. Was that too much to ask?

"Eat some oatmeal tomorrow. Half an English muffin. With pure strawberry jam," I suggested. "We'll make sure they don't put any grill on your muffin. What about that?"

Kristi drew back sharply, as if I'd pushed her head away. She looked absolutely stunned. "You know I can't do that. I thought you understood." She got up before I could grab her hand and apologize. "I thought you knew."

She might have stormed out of the room, taken a walk down the hall to chill out. But our visitors were blocking the doorway.

"Girls, I'd like you to meet Aria. She models for Doggone and Ravarge."

Mary-Alicia grinned at us. She seemed proud of her score, but we couldn't see what the fuss was about. Her sumo wrestler body blocked our view. For a minute, as she lumbered in and seated herself once more in our desk chair, I thought she was hallucinating. Maybe there was no girl with the butthole tattoo. Because the doorway remained empty.

Then the new girl appeared, making a grand entrance, striking a fashion model pose. "Hey," she whispered in this sexy rasp of a voice. Coltish, honey blonde, and conventionally pretty, the woman was dressed for the Florida nightlife. Hot pink mini, high cork heels, lots of bling. She looked wild and free, devastatingly hot.

Kristi's jaw dropped. I'm sure mine did, too.

"How's it?" Aria asked. Not caring. Not caring about anything but our stares. "You two look even weirder than Mary Alice. Wow."

"Mary-Alicia," I corrected.

But nobody heard me. They were too into Aria. I'll admit, she was totally captivating. Six feet tall with lanky legs up to there. Her lithe body was deeply tanned. She'd obviously made it to the beaches I had yet to see. But when she gave me a haughty stare, I saw at once she wasn't one of us. We were beneath her, and she would make sure all of us knew it.

"Are you here to show us your infamous tattoo?" I asked.

I was about to say something even more rude to get rid of her, to uninvite her to our hooch fest. But it was too late. Kristi was already making a mad dash for Aria. I knew what was happening. She was going to jump into the new girl's arms.

"Holy shitsky, you're here!" my tiny roomie yelled. "I've been waiting for you *all day*."

The model frowned and stepped back at once. She held up her perfectly manicured hands, stopping Kristie in her tracks.

In that smoky voice of hers, Aria warned, "Stay away from me, you crashy freak."

Freak? Ouch. I cringed.

Mary-Alicia, her face flushed with anger, said, "Hey! We don't say stuff like that here."

But Aria had already fled.

My roommate stood in the doorway, watching the model disappear down the hall. I felt her pain. Like a stab wound in the solar plexus. A hot slap across the face.

"What a hater," I said.

"Big time," Mary-Alicia acknowledged. "Told you she was bitchin'."

When Kristi finally turned around, her face was expressionless. "Shots, anyone?"

How was I supposed to guess what my roommate

was thinking? How could I see ahead to later that night when she would crush two pink tablets of Ambien into a Solo cup full of booze? How was I to know that zolpidem and alcohol can be a deadly combo?

Of course, I couldn't know all that. No lie, I am not a mind reader. I have no power to save the people I love from themselves.

Except maybe myself.

When she got out the liquor her sister had smuggled in, when she poured a little into our plastic cups, Kristi seemed fine. "That girl's a beeatch," somebody said, and we all laughed, clicked cups, drank our half-jigger of contraband. Soon after, Mary-Alicia left for her room, and my roommate and I got into our beds.

I thought she went right to sleep. I could have sworn I heard her snoring. The vodka was harsh, and it burned at the edges of my throat a while, keeping me awake. The moon was bright enough in the black night sky to lighten up the room. An owl hooted, a sad, lonely sound. The world was such an unjust place. Why did the bad children get all the toys?

I wasn't lying to myself. I wasn't in denial. I thought Kristi would be there when I awoke, tugging at my arm, telling me to hurry, we needed to get to breakfast or they might find out we'd been drinking. Kristi, upbeat, laughing. Her big dark eyes seeking mine, connecting. I really had no idea that she'd leave me. That she'd already left me.

How could you ever know a thing like that about somebody you loved?

After she'd shared the vodka that night, I'd been the one to propose the toast. "To escape!"

All three of us smiled, trying to feel a tiny spurt of hope, of good humor, maybe joy. A fleeting shot of joy.

****

In the morning, I was the one who discovered she was dead. The cup was lying on the bed beside her, and it still had dregs in it. I knew what she'd done. It was obvious.

I went for help, completely freaked. Traumatized. What the fuck? Was everybody I cared about on a mission to self-destruct? My brother. My dad. Now my roommate. When was it going to end? Hadn't I been punished enough?

After a horrendous morning full of medics, ambulances, screaming women in drab hospital pajamas, too much group counseling, and chaos, absolute chaos, I was informed I had to talk to the cops. A deep frown marring her careful mask, Mrs. Passern ushered me into a cold white conference room where I sat at a metal table across from two handsome, tanned policemen. I'm afraid I wasn't much help, so they let me go back to our room. My room. The room where Kristi had lived.

And died.

At some point, Mrs. Passern came to fetch me again, and I followed her back down the empty hall. None of the other girls came out of their rooms. It was like a morgue on our floor.

We stopped outside the conference room again. "This is mandatory whenever there's a suicide," Mrs. Passern told me in a voice whisked clean of emotion. "Those close to the victim need extra vigilance. So any thoughts of copycat behavior can be extinguished."

Okay. Like how many suicides had they

experienced at Renew, anyway? I didn't dare ask. Instead, I seated myself in the metal chair again.

I spent more useless hours with a handful of intense but ultimately unhelpful psychiatric professionals. How did I feel? How did I *feel*? My roommate was dead. Kristi was *dead!* My mind was crushed. My heart had lodged in my throat, and every beat was a painful reminder that someone I cared about was gone from my life. Forever. How did I feel? I felt like I'd always felt, only more so. Lost. Abandoned. Responsible. Guilty. Helpless. Alone. So alone.

Swirling inside myself in demented emotional circles, I kept repeating the same thing over and over to anyone who asked and some who didn't. "I didn't know they wanted to die. I didn't want any of them to die. I wanted them to live. To still be here. To talk to me, to love me."

The headshrinkers weren't getting anywhere with me. I knew that, and I didn't blame them. I hadn't gotten anywhere with me in years.

I was returned to my room where I lay on my bed. I refused medication. Fuck that, they couldn't make me. Maybe they felt sorry for me because the nurses, who were usually so insistent about meds, let it go.

Then I skipped dinner, breaking more stupid Renew rules. Again, they could have pushed it, but they didn't.

I lay there, staring at the pale pink ceiling. Yes, I'd been left behind. Once again, abandoned by someone I loved. But here's the thing I realized. *I* was still alive. *I* still had choices.

I lay there for hours, the other bed empty beside me. They'd stripped off the sheets, baring the stained mattress. The absence of my friend was a dark silence. A stark reminder of my loss and of the path not taken.

Eyes closed, mind relaxed, I spoke out loud to Kristi. "Girl, you've escaped the apparent permanence of having you in your life. I can't blame you for that. It was the choice you made, and that's your right. But you left me. It hurts. It fucking hurts."

I cried for a while. I guess I might have dozed a little.

Kristi was perched lightly beside me on my bed. She grabbed my big toe and held fast. Her face seemed brighter, and she was smiling, radiant. "Time for the quick split, my friend. Fight dirty with dirty," she advised. "The best dirty fighter wins."

I started to ask her what she meant, but Kristi put a bony index finger to her lips. She leaned forward to caress my cheek. Her tiny hand was warm, and it smelled good. Like jasmine. "Not your fault. None of it's your fault. Live your life. It's yours, Jacy. So, get to it. Go. Now."

When I opened my eyes again it was late. The halls were silent, a shaft of moonlight drifting in through the window. I checked the clock beside my bed. After two, and all quiet out on the ward.

I got out of bed, adjusting my jean shorts and wrinkled T-shirt, stepping into my flip-flops. I fetched my wallet from the bureau. Then I whispered goodbye to my roommate. I kissed her bare pillow and her stripped mattress. I patted the spot she should have been in. I patted it tenderly for a moment.

Running away was even easier than I'd imagined. I popped the screen from the window and let it fall. It landed in the bushes below with a soft rustle. I hoisted myself up and climbed onto the window ledge. It was time to go. So I went.

When I jumped out of the window, pushing myself outward and toward the lawn below, my body brushed against the bushes all the way down. Ouch. Fucking bougainvillea! I ripped the shit out of myself on the thorns. When I picked myself up off the damp grass, my bare arms were scratched and bleeding. So were the backs of my legs.

I started walking, trying to be quiet in the silent night. I wanted to appear as if I knew where I was going. But I had no idea. I'd left my duffel bag in the closet, all my clothes and the stuff I'd accumulated while at Renew. The books and magazines, the self-help reading materials. I was exiting Renew with only the beach clothes I had on and the few bucks I'd brought with me from home.

Fortunately, I also had a couple of credit cards in my wallet. Hopefully, one card would not be maxed out.

The night air was clammy and clingy. Stars glistened next door to a bulbous moon. I inhaled deeply, thrilling to my return to the outside world as I strolled as casually as possible down the manicured lawn and out the long gravel drive. Nobody stopped me, because there wasn't a soul around. So I kept going.

An owl hooted, sounding oddly encouraging. The suburban neighborhood was dark and still, the narrow streets empty of cars. Where was Tad when I needed him?

The moonlight had a silvery sheen to it, making the trees and bushes, the long ranch houses and parked cars, look glittery and day-bright. I could smell magnolia, dogwood, and other sweet blooms. Frogs croaked here and there, and once I heard a songbird trill. It was like walking through a dream.

A long, tiring dream. I trudged on and on through the empty streets, hoofing it for what felt like miles.

This place was nothing like Manhattan. Developments are a dead zone, man. Never move to the suburbs, they will fucking kill you. Nothing but sameness, cozy sameness, wherever you look. I'd go nuts living in the pink and cream tidiness of suburban Florida.

A lie, of course. Who needed geography to create insanity? Truth was, I'd already gone nuts. And I'd done so while living in the middle of the most interesting city on the planet.

I wandered up and down the cement sidewalks looking for an exit to the endless housing sameness, the cookie-cutter sprawl. I walked for hours in my damn flip-flops, all the while talking to myself in my head. I knew who I was, where I had come from, the truth about me and my fucked-up family.

At least I was trying to be honest with myself. Wasn't this progress?

Luck eventually kicked in, and I stumbled on a four-lane thoroughfare that led me to an intersection with a couple of strip malls. Pizza joints, postal center, a vintage clothing store. Deli, pool parlor, Cuban restaurant. All dark, closed for the night long ago. But there was a gas station on the corner with a phone booth. The only public phone for miles, probably.

Only I had no change on me. And the gas station wasn't open.

I sat on the curb by the gas pumps and rested my sorry feet. Dawn would break eventually, and somebody would show up, change out my dollar bills or let me use a credit card to pay for a call. Under the gas station anti-theft lighting, the asphalt glistened, oily, rainbowed.

Two of my toes were blistered, bleeding. I must have looked like hell when the Jeep pulled up, speakers blaring fun-lovin' surfer music. A kid with white-blonde hair cursed when he jumped out of the driver's seat and noticed the pumps were off.

Or maybe he swore because he spotted me sitting there. Huddled like a lost cat you don't want to take home but know you probably will.

"What the fuck?" the kid said.

His nose was bright pink like a rabbit's, the rest of his lean body tanned and smooth. He had on a pair of board shorts, bright blue with black stripes. Maybe he was sixteen, maybe not. Maybe he wasn't even old enough to drive.

"What the fuck yourself," I countered. "I need to make a phone call. You got a cell on you?"

His eyes narrowed. "Are you gonna pull some shit on me? Cuz I am not in the mood for any shit right now."

He gave me a hard stare, scratched his head. Boy oh boy, his hair was light. We don't have blonds like that in Manhattan. The sun had bleached the hell out of it.

I stood up slowly so I wouldn't scare him off. "Neither am I, bro," I promised. "I just need to call a cab. Get to the airport. You got a cell I can borrow?"

He pulled a slim phone out of a front pocket and

held it out.

I took the phone, thanked him, and made my call.

When I handed the cell back, the kid said, "Who you running away from? Messed up parents? Crappy boyfriend? Piece of shit rehab program?"

"All of the above, I guess. I'm always running away. From something." I don't know why I said that. The kid seemed harmless, and I was exhausted. Vulnerable, too. He kept looking at me, so I kept talking. "I'd like to change that about myself. Maybe find something I can commit to. But it's hard."

He scratched his head again. "Thing is, wherever you go, there you are. So you might as well get to where you wanna be with your own damn self. Me, I like the ocean." He grinned. God, his teeth were perfect. Kids these days have the best orthodontics work. "When I'm sitting out there on my board, blue all around me, gulls swooping overhead, fat mullet cruising past, waves coming in endlessly? That's life, man. *My* life."

He nodded, so I nodded back. Like I understood.

"Simple shit, but not easy shit." He dropped the phone back in his pocket. Then he waved and jumped in the front seat of the idling jeep. The dude music boomed from the tinny speakers, lyrics full of lingo about beach junkies and the love of swell and curl. Or something like that.

When he squealed out of the gas station, I waved goodbye. Then I sat down on the curb again and waited in the starlight, the moonlight, the missing darkness.

It took the cab an hour to pick me up, another one to get me to the airport.

Seven a.m., and Fort Lauderdale International was

packed. The lines were long, the airline employees cranky and hassled. Everyone seemed fidgety and rushed. That was modern life these days, the whole world like a madhouse. But after more exasperating delays you don't even want to hear about, I eventually caught an afternoon flight.

On that plane ride, I slept the whole way, dreamless and deep. I fell into an ocean of sleep and let it carry me away from shore.

Chapter Twelve

Like I told you before, I'm really good at denial. For almost a whole month after I got home, I didn't think too much about me and Firth. Even when I cuddled with Vixie, who Firth had cared for the whole time I was at Renew. He'd come by every few days to feed my cat and give him some love and attention. He brought in my mail, too, and kept the dust bunnies to a minimum. The place was cleaner than when I'd left.

I didn't think about Firth, though. Even when I ordered takeout from Joy Luck and scarfed down moo shi at the kitchen table. Not even when I relaxed with a cold beer or spotted someone with bright orange hair.

It was like I had writer's block. Only this was boyfriend block.

He didn't call me, either. Maybe it was more of a Soviet bloc. A trade embargo. Broken diplomatic relations.

I guess to compensate for my loss, or whatever, I buried myself in my work. I edited the hell out of JD's manuscript. I implanted several steaming hot sex scenes, little time bombs with fully bared tits and ass. I took them out. Right in the first chapter, I placed a handgun, a Smith & Wesson .44 Magnum, followed that up with gunplay in the middle of the book, added a fatal gunshot wound at the end. Then I took all that out, too. My manuscript was heavily redacted, and I was glad. When a book is beautifully written, you don't need gimmicks. The words speak for themselves. They sing for themselves. Story, and the language that makes it soar, are enough.

One dark spring afternoon, I stood up from my computer and stretched my limbs until my hip joints popped. I looked at Vixie. "Fuck it, friend. I am *tout finis*." I kind of liked how it sounded, so I added, "*Très bien*."

He turned from his perch at the window, his tail flitting around behind his sleek little head. I swear to you, my cat gave me the stink eye.

"*Tout finit par se savoir*," the cat said. "Either you call old Firth and tell him everything, or I will." Vixie's voice was quite stern. There was no trace of a mellow meow in his tone.

I laughed at him. "Go ahead, cat. Give the big man a call. See if you get any catnip cookies after that."

Vixie licked his chops, yawned, and looked away. His tail crooked at the top, wavering, like he was pointing it at me. He said nothing more on the subject.

But after that, I thought about Firth a lot more. Missed him. Wanted his brawny arms around me, my sad face against his wide, furry chest. I wanted a truce. How about détente? But I was afraid to call him. What would I say? That part of me was a liar? That one of my various selves had lied, but I wasn't sure which one?

I submitted my manuscript to JD's former literary agency with a carefully worded cover letter that made no mention of the ghostwriting relationship. Then I had a chat with Mitch, my boss, who seemed thrilled to put me back on the schedule. He liked having me there, he said; my sassy style pleased the bar's regular customers. Maybe Mitch was hot for me, I don't really know. I didn't pick up on it if he was. I wasn't into it with him or any other guy. I still had it bad for old Firth, I guess.

Working seven nights a week kept my head out of the dirty cesspool. I liked the income, too. I actually saved enough cash to pay the rent that month. Without any help from Mother for a change. Which was lucky, because she'd failed to mail me a check in time. That kind of oversight wasn't like her, but the timing was good. I would have been evicted if she'd ever missed a payment when I was unable to cover it on my own. But she never had.

****

It was a busy night at work when I got the call. I was running my ass off, so I didn't answer my phone. After I'd finished serving burgers and beers to a table of rowdy real estate brokers, I went to the ladies room to check my messages. Mitch didn't want us on the phone while we were waiting on customers. I agreed. Don't you just hate it when you're ordering food or buying a product or whatever, and the cashier or waiter is ignoring you and yakking away on their cell?

Anyway, the missed call was from the NYPD. Cops? Couldn't be good news. I called back, my heart breakdancing around in my chest.

After a series of operators and a series of annoying holds, I hung up on the NYPD telephone maze and went back to work. Fuck it. If it was that important, they'd call me again later.

On my way home that night, I checked my phone. The night was warm with a certain softness, the kind of hint you get in spring that reminds you how close to summer it is. I unzipped my hoodie, sauntering up Eighth as I listened to a glut of messages. Ads, reminders to pay certain bills—fuck those college loan bastards—a bunch of rude shake-downs from a really aggressive credit card company. Nobody I wanted to listen to. I almost erased the whole lot of them, then I remembered the NYPD. So I listened to the rest.

One was from Aunt Jane, my mother's sister. Those two didn't speak. They'd had a big fight many years back. So as soon as Aunt Jane said my name, I knew what was coming. I stood still and held my breath.

"Jacy, I have bad news," my aunt's message began. "The police have been trying to reach you. They were over at the house on West 87th."

Mother was dead.

The world around me shifted. It was like the opposite of being wasted. All my cells lined up and everything inside my head began to unravel. Old tapes snapped, disconnecting, worn pathways dissolving in thick clouds of rust-colored dirt. A bell in my head clanged. Something was over—a round, a class, a chess game. A phase of my life. My body, my whole being, felt solid all of a sudden, grounded in the place where I stood. This cement sidewalk. This hectic block of this hectic city. This particular moment. Me, just me, in this body. Breathing the cool night air, standing under the invisible stars, listening to my own heart beating, still beating. Me, my life. *This* life.

Maybe denial world disappeared at that very moment, I don't know. Only time will tell. But what I can say for sure is this. I suddenly remembered everything that happened the night I met Firth. How depressed I'd been. The shots of Stoli, followed by the brown-bag with spiked Red Bull, the endless rounds of foamy draft beers. I recalled distinctly why I was hitting it so hard, and what I'd said to the big Irish-looking guy sitting next to me at the bar.

"My brother's anniversary is today," was what I said, only with a slur so it sounded like my brothersh annie-ver-shary'sh today. "He died four years ago today. Right before his eighteenth birthday. Suicide. An incredible kid, so much potential. It killed my family, absolutely destroyed us." Dee-shtroy-ed ush.

The guy beside me reached over and put one large hand on my back, patting me gently. "Wow, that sucks. That really sucks."

I could see in his clear calm eyes that he meant it. That he knew about suffering, and how it helped to talk about it.

"That's so fucken terrible," my new friend said. "What happened?"

I never talked about this. My brother's death. I just kept it deep inside where it festered like a hidden wound. But there was something about my drunken state and the genuine concern of the big warm man next to me that made me relax. And open up that old wound. There seemed to be a chance for me to allow the air, the time that had passed, the balm of a stranger's genuine interest to do some healing on that old wound. Or at least that was how I felt when I decided, in my drunken state, to share the truth.

"He hung himself," I said. "In his bedroom."

"Fer fuck's sake. Goddam."

I loved the passion of my drinking buddy's reactions. This opened me up even more. So I told him the whole story. How it happened and what happened after.

Jerome had always been intense. Intensely smart, intensely driven, intensely himself. He wasn't an easy person to get along with because his focus was so narrow. Even as a small child, he was always asking questions. Observing the world, studying it, analyzing everything. He was a math whiz and could program computers by age seven. My parents were so proud of him. A certified genius. And he was sweet, a nice kid.

Then he discovered chess. Once he learned the game, he became obsessed. He lived and breathed chess.

My dad took him to tournaments all over the city. He won some events in his age group, and top ranked players took notice. They said he had talent, an unusual way of looking at the board. They advised my dad to hire a chess coach.

The coach told my parents Jerome had the kind of mind that could take him far with the game. He agreed to come to West 87th Street to give my brother chess lessons every day. School took a back seat, then no seat. Everything else was forgotten in Jerome's single-minded drive to be the best. Jerome didn't do any more homework, he didn't play sports, and he didn't watch TV. He studied chess. He played chess. He dreamed chess, too, probably.

And he was good. Very good. He began to get attention, first in the local chess clubs, then in the press. He was high rated for his age. He was high rated for any age. By age thirteen he was a master. He wanted to go higher. International master. Grandmaster. World champion.

He got chess scholarships to travel to national events. Then to international events. By age fifteen, he had been all over the world. Paris. Budapest. Dublin. Johannesburg. Rio. Mexico City. Moscow. Sarajevo. Linares. He was on the road all the time. When he came home, he was exhausted. Thin. Pale. Unhealthy and nervous. He paced his room. He talked to himself. He slept a lot.

Frightened for my brother's mental health, I read up on the topic. Chess players, what were they like? I read about Bobby Fischer. That guy was a real head case. My brother seemed comparatively normal for a kid playing so much chess. He was simply living the strange and intense life of a professional chess player.

But he was so young and his standards were so high. He'd set the bar way up there. He wanted to be one of the top players in the world, and nothing else would do. It's extraordinarily difficult. Once you are high rated, your competition is really good. They can be unbeatable, some of them. They're as intense and driven and as gifted as you are. Maybe more so.

My brother's advancement stalled. He couldn't boost his rating, he couldn't pass the norms required to become a grandmaster. He became depressed. And then suicidal. That was when he was sixteen.

My mother stepped in. She took him to a doctor, who hospitalized him for thirty days. When he came out of the private sanitarium, he was like a shell of his former self. The intensity was gone. He shuffled around my parents' apartment, hunched over, inward looking, his eyes downcast. He told me all the medications clouded his mind.

After that, Jerome stopped playing chess. He quit

just like that. He said he couldn't play chess anymore. Not well enough to compete anyway.

That's when he turned into a recluse. No more tournaments, no more chess clubs, no more travel. He was only seventeen, and he rarely came out of his room.

And then it happened. He was home alone one day. I was in college, so I was not privy to his condition. I didn't know how bleak he'd become. My dad was out at the airport or chauffeuring somebody to or from the city. And my mother? She'd gone shopping. Clothes shopping. Neiman was having a sale.

When she came home, loaded down with shopping bags, my brother was dead. His face had already turned blue. Blackened blue. His body was cold. Ice cold.

Mother called nine one one. When I got a call and rushed home, he was already gone. To the morgue. To the funeral home. To another place.

My father collapsed, but Mother was strong. She told me we had to be tough. We had to keep our cool. Yes, the loss hurt terribly. Yes, we would miss him. But we had to carry on. Keep our heads up. Maintain our direction.

I was a good girl back then. I did as I was told.

"That must have been devastating. What a burden. And you were only a kid, too," my new friend said.

He said all the right things, this guy.

Drunk, torn wide open, I went on and on about it. I'm an absolute madwoman when I'm drunk. Take my word. I rambled on about my father's debilitating depression over the loss of his only son. Selling his taxi medallion once he could no longer work. Hiding in the basement, pretending he could invent something to make all our problems disappear. Me finding him there, the gun beside him. The weird smell of the blood. Blackened blood mixed with cordite, or gunpowder, whatever sulfuric chemical it is that dusts the air after a weapon is fired. Whatever a firearm leaves behind in addition to all that blood. In addition to the permanence of loss, of untimely death. Me standing there, helpless, staring down at my dad's body. His chest blown away, a gaping wound in place of a heart.

"Shit, that must have been so fucken awful," my new friend said. He was still patting me. I liked the way his huge palm fit over the small of my back. "How did you handle it, being just a kid and losing the people you loved most?"

How did I handle it? I'd never handled it. What was the opposite of handling your pain? Denying it.

I tried to explain about my mother and her insistence that we appear normal. How we had to present a united, false front to the rest of the world. No sense dwelling on our losses. We had to be strong, carry on, act like we were fine.

My new friend nodded. "That's how a lot of families deal with grief." He shook his head, lifted his beer mug. "That's what this shite is for, right?"

We drank more beer as I rattled on and on. About how I dropped out of grad school and moved out of my childhood home. Moved to my own place, a dumpette in Midtown. Thrilled to be on my own but still struggling and desperately alone. In some kind of black mood, I went out and bought a bunch of second-hand furnishings. A lot of black stuff. I lay on top of the black cotton sheets, the black afghan. Recovering or trying to.

Maybe it was my blue period. Whatever. I went

from black to blue and back again. The therapist I saw uptown prescribed Klonopin and later Abilify. On top of the Adderall, the Lexapro. I took what I wanted when I wanted. Except for a party high, I wasn't really into all those zombie pills.

My drinking buddy kept nodding, encouraging me to tell him the rest. All of it. Spill, spill.

I kept talking. I explained how I eventually made myself get up, get out, get the waitressing job. I eased back into the world that way, which gradually made me feel more alive. Then I began to really liven things up. I pushed myself, then I stopped holding myself back. I ended up going a little wild. Flirting, fighting, fucking around. At night, I frequented the hellholes. Dumpster diving. Swimming in sewers. I knew it was insane. What was also nuts was how I kept trying to write. Even though it made me even crazier. Because it wasn't going anywhere.

A metaphor. I wasn't going anywhere, either.

"I work with a lot of people who've suffered trauma," my bar friend told me. "You're one of the bravest I've ever met. You're so honest. The way you accept your past. Deal with your sorrow. That makes you one of the strongest people I know."

I might have thrown up a little bit after that.

The guy was cool about it, he told me his name was Firth and he lived nearby. He said we could go to his place and sober up. We went to his cold, dank apartment, and to stay warm, climbed into bed together. He held me close. We talked for hours. If somebody at least listens to you, then your life feels less awful.

Early the next morning, I woke up in Firth's arms. But my head wasn't in the same place it had been the night before. Sober, I was back in denial world. I ran out of there like I had a real life to rush back to. I didn't. I'm a terrific liar. But one thing I couldn't lie to myself about—I liked this guy.

Firth. Big, beautiful, warrior man Firth.

So yeah, I met him in a bar. So what? We had a few drinks, and I told him about my fucked-up life, my wildly dysfunctional family, my personal history of insanity and poor choices. Still, he thought I was interesting. Worth getting to know. Worth caring about.

When I got back to my apartment on that warm night in June, I peeled off my hoodie and plopped down on the couch. Vixie jumped into my lap, licked my chin, and settled in for a brief period of mutual affection. I sat there petting his sleek black fur until he purred. He kneaded my thighs, rubbing up against my hand, loving me in his independent cat way until I finally stopped crying.

With my free hand, I speed-dialed Firth. He sounded groggy. But he'd answered on the second ring. Even though it was after midnight. Even though it was me.

"I want a real relationship," I said. "My mother's dead. Can you come over?"

"Sure," he said. "How many Guinnies you got?"

Turns out I had enough for two.

Epilogue

You already know a lot of the rest. The rest of my
story. Although, so much of what was in the
newspapers and all over the Internet was exaggerated.
But the bones of it were there.

Let me put some meat on it for you.

JD's former literary agency signed me up. They
sold the book instantly for six figures. They sold it to
one of those premier, snobby-assed New York
publishing houses that have monopolized the industry
for a hundred years. Almost immediately, I was
featured in *PW*, *The Times* book review, and on all the
top lit blogs. Everybody wanted a piece of me. A young
woman who wrote like JD? Who claimed she'd
channeled the late great novelist for her first novel?
Wow. The media sat up and begged.

My book was a sure-fire bestseller, everyone
predicted. Destined to become a major hit, a
blockbuster movie, a classic.

But then JD's relatives got wind of the novel. They
said I didn't have the right to use his characters in my
book. Even though their dead relative had dictated the
story to me, which of course they neither accepted nor
understood. Not that I blamed them. It was, after all,
completely insane. And they had attorneys.

It didn't take long for the publisher to drop me. My
agency, which was supposed to protect me from all this

legal crap, stopped returning my frantic calls. They wouldn't even email me. Overnight, as quickly as I'd become the hot new novelist in town, I was suddenly publishing poison. I went from it girl to shit girl in the wink of an ironic eye.

Throughout all this, there was no sign of JD. I thought he might pop up, give me some encouragement. Then I thought maybe he was taking a new tack, trying to talk sense to his relatives. Or maybe he'd jumped my sinking ship and decided to work with one of his kids on our project. Maybe he was attempting to prevent them from releasing his other unpublished manuscripts. The ones he'd said were crap.

Whatever he was up to, JD was no longer in my life. He was obviously done with me.

It would have been so easy to drink, drug, and crack up into all my former parts. I could have spun out, flipping myself like an old pancake, sizzling in the hot grease of madwoman oblivion. Again.

Instead, I bucked up. Sat right down and hacked out another novel.

And yes indeed, I channeled this one, too. Once again, I allowed the voice to speak through me. But this time, it didn't belong to my ghost writer. It wasn't JD's dictation I was listening to. No, this time what I was listening to was my own voice. The other Jacy, the part of me I'd been denying for so long.

I sat there at my computer for hours, transcribing whatever the hell I had to say to myself. About my own life, my fucked-up family. Only I fictionalized it, made it kooky and sweet, full of philosophical tidbits. Turned out I was pretty entertaining. Insightful. Funny. A heck of a storyteller, and a darn good writer.

Who knew?

I liked it, writing that way. Writing in my own voice. In fact, I kind of loved it. I went in deeper and deeper. I explored life. My life. Because that's what I'd chosen to do. Write.

My fingers loped across the keyboard until the day I turned to Vixie and said, "Kit-cat, I am *tout fini*."

Vixie twitched his sexy whiskers. His crooked tail switched back and forth. We stared at one another.

But my cat did not respond this time. He did not lecture me, scold me about how the truth will out. He kept his thoughts to himself, returning to his vigil at the window.

I hunted down my old binoculars and stood beside the mesmerized cat, staring down into the alley below. Dumpsters, all sorts of trash spilling from cans and scattered about. Plastic bags skittering in the wind. Whatever was Vixie looking at? I guess I will never know.

My shit girl status was short-lived. The first agency I submitted my new manuscript to jumped on it. Only because they recognized my name, of course. For fifteen minutes, I'd been a bad girl celeb. Like Britney or Lindsay. Miley. Madonna.

So my first novel is out now and, as you know, the book is a massive hit. Twenty-nine weeks on all the major bestseller lists. And counting. *The Times* loved it. So did the *Observer*. Facebook, Twitter, Goodreads and Amazon, all the book review websites, I am virtually everywhere. NPR. Charlie Rose. Not Oprah, not yet. But you never know.

I don't enjoy this part of the writer's job. All the press, I mean. Don't get me started on the self-promotion bullshit you have to do with a bestselling book. It's intolerable. But necessary. I'm all over it. I'm insufferable.

JD must be rolling in his grave.

If I knew where he was buried, I'd go visit my old ghost friend. I'd love to see Vermont anyway, and he's somewhere on the border there, near New Hampshire. It would be fun to be the one to write "fuck you" on his gravestone. Like he always expected somebody to do. But I haven't been invited.

Hey, JD shouldn't be avoiding me. He should be thanking me. My agent informed me last week that sales of JD's books have received a secondary bounce. From my publicity, my book sales. The pervy old ghost writer should be grateful, right? Because I'm introducing more readers to JD Balinger's work. That's a good thing all around. The world can only benefit from reading all of the late great's work. He was the master, capturing perfectly the humor and pain of youth angst. Something we all need to understand. And learn from. So, thanks to me, JD, who never goes out of style, is experiencing renewed attention in the public discourse.

After all, that's what writers work to achieve— popular success. An ongoing fan base. Generation after generation of readers who care. Discriminating readers who devour our books, inhaling our words, breathing them in like cool fresh air. Reading our books and saying, "Beautiful. This is just plain beautiful."

That's really all I want to say. I'd end this right here, but I can't. I know you. Because you're such a romantic, you want to know what happened with me and Firth.

As JD once said, "It's beautiful the way loose ends find each other in the world."

Firth, the dear heart, came right over after I found out Mother had died. He stood by me through her funeral and everything. The service was small—us, the Ivaneks, and their nurse. A few tenants from the other floors also came by to pay their respects. And Aunt Jane in her Lilly Pulitzer shift and pale green espadrilles, looking way too much like Mrs. Passern for my taste, showed up for the funeral, too.

Okay, so maybe the service wasn't that small. Anyway, it was nice. I sent lilacs. Women appreciate flowers, even when they're dead.

Mr. Ivanek was the one who'd called the police. He said he heard strange noises coming from upstairs. He thought she'd fallen and couldn't get up. Actually, Mother had collapsed. The medical examiner said she died of cardiac arrest due to malnutrition. That woman never ate enough.

Turns out Mother was broke. Between me, Daddy, and Jerome, the years of medical bills for our poor mental health had done her in. She'd refinanced the apartment, never once hinting to me about her worsening financial situation. She could have saved herself a lot of problems by putting the apartment on the market. But she held on. Right to the very end.

I sold the place on West 87th Street for megabucks. Mother had been counting pennies while living in a multi-million dollar property. You want to get rich? Don't kill yourself trying to write a lousy book. Get into Manhattan real estate instead. Holy shitsky.

Anyway, after I paid off Mother's debt and got rid of the college loan sharks—go to hell, you scum-suckers—I wanted to do something with all that I'd been given. A major book deal, valuable real estate, the freedom to live a singular life. I had the urge to give back. To provide something worthwhile to folks who might be having a hard time with growing up. Dealing with dysfunctional families. Trying to cope with the pain of becoming a whole person.

So I talked to Firth about it. He suggested we see somebody. Work out our shit, see if we could make a go of it. Then maybe do something together. Start a foundation or something.

"You and me starting a foundation is a fine idea. But see a fucking therapist?" I shouted. "No fucking way."

How could he even suggest something like that? He'd heard my horror stories about Renew. I'd told him about my overanalyzed brother, my overmedicated dad. How much good had the zombie pills done any of us? None. Wasn't the psychiatric route just a death march?

"Are you kidding me?" I slammed my mug on the bar, sloshing pale ale.

"No, and I'm not fucken around," he said. "I want to be your family, Jacy. Your sane family."

That stopped me for a second. Then, as I opened my mouth to argue the point, Firth, god love him, leaned over and kissed me. I melted. That man had the most pillowy lips.

A few minutes later, we left Collie's arm in arm. The night was warm and smelled of fish. I swear, the ocean lapped at the edges of the city. Even with my heavy cowboy boots on, I rode some kind of wave all the way back to my place.

We kissed in the lobby, in my foyer, up against the

wall of the hallway. We kissed slowly, languidly, then fiercely. Maybe it was the drink, but I lost myself in him that night. I let go, and we washed out to sea.

We tumbled down the hall to my bedroom. Street light trickled in, casting Firth in a golden glow. When Vixie leaped off the bed and fled, my big man laughed. I caught his laugh, his contagious laugh. Both smiling, we undressed one another slowly, carefully, like we were stepping out of our most delicate skin.

As Firth made love to me, I swam right through him. His tenderness, the way he held me so lightly, like a starfish in the palm of the sea. Whenever I opened my eyes, he was looking at me. He saw me. He loved me. And it was okay. I fell into him, into us.

Later, when we were lying around on my bed, sweaty, salty and sated like we'd just crawled out of the Atlantic after a long swim, I said, "You win." I promised Firth I would do whatever it took. No quick splits. Because I wasn't going to lose him. I wasn't going to lose us.

The Tao of us.

Firth found us this fantastic family therapist in Harlem, a down to earth guy with a goatee and a giggle. He helped us wade through the things that were holding us back. I dumped all the party meds, we both reduced our alcohol intake, and we made us work. We talked and talked. We loved one another. We were family.

Last spring, after the baby was born, Firth and I set up a couple of scholarship-based after-school programs. Free chess lessons, taught by some of the city's most skilled young players. And creative writing classes, taught by some of the area's most talented young writers. All the teachers in the McMaster Programs are well paid. They deserve it.

Firth loves being a dad. He's really good with little Jerry. He's also really good to me. He still has to remind me how the truth isn't just one thing, how it evolves. He's always telling me that the truth is like your life—it's something you have to work at every day.

Sometimes I forget. We still fight over stuff. I could go on and on about the kind of shit we argue over. Like how I think JD was real, not just some part of my brain, crazed and on the loose. How my brother, too, was really there, in his room playing chess, all those years. I believe there's a kind of reality to that. And sometimes such realities can be more real than our everyday life. Daddy, hanging around down in the basement where he took his own life? Sure, why not?

I know, I know. We've established that my faculties are not always a hundred percent intact. I can be a real madwoman sometimes. But I'm not the only one who's open to *Twilight Zone* stuff like this. The existence of an alternate world, another level of reality? A world as real as ours, sometimes overlapping ours? It's certainly possible. We don't know everything, right?

But somebody stop me, please. I could blah, blah, blah about this stuff forever, like I do when Firth and I have one of our endless discussions. To tell you the truth, we see life very differently. The way I see it is, your life is a symbol. Everything you do is part of the pattern you make. If you're one of the sheeple, you let other people make the pattern and you just fit yourself in, following along. Baa, baa. Bleat, bleat.

I don't know what the hell else to say about it.

Except this—Firth told me sheep were once wild and adventurous, strong-willed animals that ran around on their own. Humans bred them to be the way they are now, herd animals, docile, fearful little wool factories. With a hive mind. Doing what all the other wooly guys are doing. People can be the same way. People tend to be like that, is what I mean to say. But I don't want to go into all that right now. I really don't feel like it, so I won't.

Maybe some other time.

About the Author

Mickey J. Corrigan writes crazy romance and sexy psychological thrillers. Her stories have been called "delightful pulp," "oh so compulsive" reads, and "bizarre but believable." Recent books include the mad love series *The Hard Stuff*, and two darkly romantic crime capers, *The Blow Off* and *Ex-Treme Measures*, all from The Wild Rose Press, Inc.

~*~

Visit Mickey at

http://www.mickeyjcorrigan.com

~*~

To chat with Mickey J. Corrigan and other Wild Rose Press authors, join us at

www.groups.yahoo.com/group/thewildrosepress.